"Where's my daughter?" Missy asked, hating the huskiness of her voice.

Liam moved to the edge of the porch. Despite the passage of time, he looked the same, like an older version of the boy she'd known. He was impossibly handsome in jeans, a long-sleeved dress shirt with the cuffs folded back to his elbows and cowboy boots.

Always cowboy boots.

His gaze lit on her, but the setting sun and deep shadows of the porch made it impossible to see his expression as he thanked the driver who'd placed her suitcases on the porch. She tore her gaze from him and thanked the man as well when he walked past her. When it was just the two of them again, she returned her focus to Liam, who hadn't moved other than to cross his arms over his chest.

The defensive pose spoke volumes about his state of mind.

Fine, but right now she wanted to see for herself that Casey was okay. "I asked you—"

"Is it true?" The words were out of his mouth as she reached for the stair railing, freezing her on the first step. "Is Casey my daughter?" he demanded.

* * *

Welcome to Destiny:
Where fate leads to falling in love

Dear Reader,

Some say one moment can change your life forever. Liam Murphy has learned this firsthand based on a couple of occurrences in his life—the loss of his first love, the end of a promising rodeo career—but nothing prepared him for what happens when he's told he's a father...by a fifteen-year-old girl claiming to be his daughter.

It's a stunning revelation to say the least, and when the girl's mother, his high school sweetheart, arrives in Destiny to explain how this could be possible, Liam's smart enough to realize his life is never going to be the same again.

Missy Dobbs knows this is true as well for her, but she's determined to do what's best for her daughter. Even if that means practically living under the same roof with her old love while he and their daughter get to know each other. Only, she's finding herself falling for the man Liam is now.

They are a family, yes, but could they be more? Can Missy put her heart on the line once again? Maybe this time she and Liam will find they are destined to be together.

Writing this different twist on the classic secret baby trope was a lot of fun, and I hope you enjoy reading about the latest Murphy brother finding his happily-ever-after.

All the best,

Christyne

Destined to Be a Dad

Christyne Butler

———

HARLEQUIN® SPECIAL EDITION®

Recycling programs
for this product may
not exist in your area.

ISBN-13: 978-0-373-65909-8

Destined to Be a Dad

Printed in U.S.A.

www.Harlequin.com

Christyne Butler is a *USA TODAY* bestselling author who fell in love with romance novels while serving in the US Navy and started writing her own stories in 2002. She writes contemporary romances that are full of life, love and a hint of laughter. She lives with her family in central Massachusetts and loves to hear from her readers at christynebutler.com.

Visit the Author Profile page at Harlequin.com for more titles.

To the following extraordinary authors...
you have no idea how much your books mean to me,
as a fan who spends many hours
lost in the pleasure of reading them
and as a writer for the inspiration you provide.
Thank you!

Donna Alward
Rachel Gibson
Kristan Higgins
Shirley Jump
Virginia Kantra
Laura Kaye
Susan Mallery
Catherine Mann
Sarah Morgan
Molly O'Keefe
Christine Rimmer
Jill Shalvis
Roxanne St. Claire
Karen Templeton

Chapter One

"Wankers! You cowboys promised to take me to Liam Murphy, not show me the back side of some bloody barn!"

The lilting British accent, rarely heard here in the small town of Destiny, Wyoming, floated on the hot August morning breeze. It came from somewhere behind him and despite the voices bickering on the other end of this endless phone call—and the fact she'd said his name—the inflection kicked Liam square in the gut.

He should have been used to it by now.

His family's business, Murphy Mountain Log Homes, was celebrating its twentieth year in business with a growing following in the United Kingdom, thanks to securing a contract to build a log home—scratch that, a twenty-thousand-square-foot log mansion—for a popular movie actor based in Scotland.

Meaning as company president, Liam spent a lot of time on the phone and in meetings with people who spoke the

Queen's English. Still, whenever he heard that soft and silvery accent spoken by a female voice, it never failed to take him back.

To another place, another time when he'd thought he could have it all.

Aw, hell, that was a lifetime ago.

"Are you daft?" The girlish voice came again, cutting into Liam's thoughts. "Not bloody happening!"

Hmm, not so soft this time.

She sounded young and her words were angry, but there was a hint of fear laced through as well. Liam didn't know what was going on, but he had a pretty good idea.

Ending his call, he pocketed his phone, backtracked a few steps and headed for the far end of a nearby barn.

The first-ever Destiny rodeo was in full swing, and campers and horse trailers filled this area of the fairgrounds. It'd taken a lot of hard work by a lot of people to pull this event together. His family's company was a major sponsor, and while it might only be a one-day event, the prize money was good, ensuring participants and fans alike packed the arena and the town.

The last thing they needed was trouble.

Liam spotted the trio as soon as he rounded the corner. Dressed in jeans, plaid shirts and Stetsons, two cowboys stood with a young girl sandwiched between them. He wasn't sure about the men, but the female definitely looked to be under eighteen. That made the six-pack of beer held by one of the cowboys—who didn't have a valid alcohol wristband—even more of a concern. And it wasn't even noon yet.

"Come on, darlin'. Let's enjoy a cold brew in our camper." One of the cowboys encircled the girl's waist with his arm. "Then we'll track down that Murphy guy for ya."

"No need to go far." Liam kept his voice light as he

strolled toward the group, despite his anger spiking at the scene before him. "I'm right here."

The three jerked around, surprise on the faces of the cowboys, relief in the girl's eyes. And there was something else about their dark navy coloring that hit him as hard as her voice had.

"What can I help you with?" he continued, joining their circle. "Something related to the rodeo, perhaps?"

The first cowboy took a step back, dropping his hold on the young girl, whose gaze darted from the booklet she held to Liam and back again. Twice.

Liam looked down and saw she had the rodeo program folded back to the pages that featured his photo. Great. That's why she was looking for him.

He and his brothers had all grown up on horseback, competing in local rodeos before they were even teenagers. But it'd been Liam who'd made it to the professional circuit as a saddle bronc rider when he'd turned eighteen, finishing in the top five at the National Rodeo Finals his first two years out. His third—and what would end up being his final—season had ended early when he destroyed his left shoulder. He never rode professionally again.

That had been thirteen years ago.

When the Destiny rodeo committee had wanted him for the cover of the program based on his past accomplishments, he'd balked but finally given in and agreed to be included inside, never thinking they'd make him a damn centerfold.

"Ah, Mr. Murphy, we were j-just looking for you," the younger of the two cowboys said.

So now he was Mr. Murphy. Well, that could work in his favor. "What's with the beer?" Liam gestured at the kid with the six-pack under his arm. "You're not twenty-one."

"I, um…"

"It's mine. He's carrying it for me," said the taller cowboy, giving his left hand a quick shake before he dropped his hands to his side and planted his feet in a wide stance. "We're on our way back to our camper."

Liam turned, picking up on the wristband and the attitude. At thirty-four, the last thing he needed was a roll in the dirt with a kid more than a decade younger than him. "Then I suggest you carry it. Be less trouble that way."

Their gazes held for a long moment, but the cowboy backed down, making a show of taking the alcohol, and then slapped the younger guy on the shoulder. "Come on, bro. Let's get out of here."

Liam watched them leave, making a mental note to check in with the sheriff. Gage Steele and his deputies were patrolling the fairgrounds, but Liam hadn't seen anyone back this way yet.

He turned his attention back to the girl. Shoulder-length blond hair, streaked with bright patches of blue and pink, fell over her face as she stood studying the program again. "Are you okay?" he asked. "They didn't hurt you?"

She lifted her gaze, her eyes raking from the top of his Stetson to the tips of his boots before she looked him in the eye. "Are you really him?"

A bit uncomfortable at her scrutiny, Liam looked at where she jabbed a finger at the picture of his winning ride that first year. "Yes, but that was a long time ago." He spotted a small duffel bag lying nearby in the grass. Moving past her, he grabbed it. "Is this yours?"

"Yeah, thanks."

He watched her walk toward him, studying her again and wondering if there might be another reason she'd been looking for him. She was pretty, if one got past the crazy-colored hair, dark eye makeup and…was that a diamond chip on the side of her nose?

She had a slew of earrings dangling from both ears, her black T-shirt displayed a bright purple skull surrounded by flowers and she wore skintight jeans tucked into brown leather boots accented with bright turquoise embroidery that looked new.

Brand-new, from the way she hobbled. "You buy those today?"

She nodded, looking at her feet. "Not hard to spot, huh? They hurt bloody awful."

Her accent pulled at him again, making him frown. "The vendor should've given you a pair of boot socks."

"They did." She shrugged. "But I already had socks. See?"

Balancing on one foot, she tried to pull the other from inside the boot but gasped, a wince creasing her features, and she froze.

"I think we should get you to the first-aid tent," Liam said, looking at the row of vendors not too far away. The tent set up by the local clinic was at the end closest to them. "Can you make it there?"

"Do I have a choice?" She yanked the bag from his grip and started to shuffle across the grass, the frightened girl from moments ago long gone. "Last time I listen to an American cowboy. They're all a bunch of nutters."

"Not all of us." Liam joined her, grinning at her quick-silver mood change. She reminded him of his niece, Abby, who had turned sixteen earlier this year. His older brother had his hands full with that one, not to mention his twin sons, who were a few years younger. "You need to be more careful who you make friends with."

"Ya think? Jeez, you sound just like my—oh!" She stumbled, one boot catching on a rock, but she caught herself before ending up on her backside. "Bollocks! That hurt!"

"Can I make another suggestion?"

She pushed her hair off her face, swiping hard at one eye before glaring at him. "Sure, why not?"

Liam's chest tightened at the tear she hadn't managed to brush away. "How about I give you a lift? The sooner we get your foot looked at, the better you'll feel."

"A lift?" Her brows scrunched together over the top of her nose in a way that was so familiar, Liam could only stare. Before he could decide why, understanding dawned on her face. Her expression turned disbelieving. "You mean carry me?"

"If that would be all right with you."

She hugged her bag to her chest and studied him again.

Damn, maybe that wasn't such a good idea. More and more people were milling around the vendor tents. He'd already spotted a few giving the two of them some speculative looks. Gossip was a favorite pastime in Destiny, and the Murphy family always seemed to supply plenty of fodder, whether they wanted to or not.

The town was still buzzing over Liam's brother Devlin taking off to London back in June with his newest lady love, a girl he'd only known a few months.

Then three weeks ago, both Liam and Nolan had participated in a bachelor auction to raise money for the town's summer camp. The fact that Liam had gone for one of the highest bids to nearby Laramie's pretty city attorney had actually ended up in the local newspaper. Good thing they hadn't gotten wind of their date last week—which had been nice but spark-free—or else that would've made the headlines as well.

"Okay." She shrugged with a feigned carelessness that reminded him again of his niece.

Liam smiled, forgetting about the crowd. There was so much going on at today's events, he doubted anyone would even notice them during the short stroll to the first-aid tent. Seconds later, he had one arm beneath her knees and the other secured just beneath her shoulders.

Cradling her bag in her lap, she wrapped the other hand around his neck as he started walking. "Do I weigh a lot?" she asked.

Liam resisted the urge to roll his eyes. No matter the age, the female species never stopped asking loaded questions. "Of course not. I bet you don't weigh a hundred pounds."

"Forty-four kilos."

He did the math in his head. "Ninety-seven pounds. See? I was right."

"For a Yank you did that conversion pretty fast."

She smiled and that punch to his gut returned. "Well, I'm a pretty smart guy."

Ducking her head, she whispered, "I hope so."

Having no idea what she meant by that, Liam covered the distance to the tent in a matter of minutes and once inside, placed the girl on an empty chair. It took one of the volunteers a few moments to tend to the blisters on her feet. Liam used that time to study her again, positive now that he knew her from someplace. But where? Could she be a friend of his niece's or a daughter of one of the guys on his construction crew? With that accent?

"You're staring at me."

Liam blinked, realizing she was right. "Ah, sorry. You know, you never did say why you were looking for me."

She tugged her boots back on, over a thick pair of socks this time, her gaze darting around the tent. Other than a few people at the far end, they were alone.

"Do I look familiar to you?" she finally asked. "At all?"

"You…" His voice trailed off. He had a feeling she

wanted him to say yes. He almost did, but the truth was he had no idea who she was. "No, I'm sorry, you don't."

She heaved a dramatic sigh and then rooted around inside her duffel bag, digging out a cell phone. "Bloody thing is about out of juice, but maybe…" Her fingers flew over the screen, her thumb flipping through a long string of photos before she turned the phone to him.

"How about her?" she asked. "Does *she* look familiar?"

His breath disappeared. Every muscle in his body tensed and his knees automatically locked to keep him upright.

Stay back, stiff rein, set feet, squeeze and stay on.

Liam had created his own personal mantra back when he was a teenager, and he silently recited those words every time he climbed on the back of a horse.

A horse determined to buck him off and send him crashing to the dirt.

A lot of people thought saddle bronc riding was only about trying to hang on. It wasn't. There were specific locations a rider's feet needed to be from the moment the chute gate opened if one expected to last the required eight seconds to garner a score.

It was a perfectly choreographed dance of man working to remain synchronized with each twist and turn and jump the horse made. All while keeping his free hand from touching the animal or himself so he wasn't disqualified.

Now, that same chant raced through his head as he stared at a picture of Missy Ellington, his very own heartbreak girl.

Missy had come over as an exchange student from London during his senior year of high school, and from the moment he'd first seen her, he'd fallen hard.

And she'd been just as smitten with him. They'd been inseparable until things ended badly the summer after graduation. A nasty fight over each other's plans for their shared future. Plans they had never bothered to talk about, plans that had turned out to be vastly different. He'd said some stupid things and the next thing he knew, Missy had flown home to London.

He never saw or spoke to her again. He thought about her sometimes though. An old country song would come on the radio, or he'd catch a whiff of a peach-scented perfume or hear a woman speak in a British accent.

And back in the spring, when Devlin had made a crack about Liam's dismal track record at marriage and how a long-ago girlfriend had been the love of his life, Liam had quickly corrected him, stating emphatically that he had no such love.

He'd been lying. She had been the love of his life, at least back then.

In the photograph, Missy looked much as she had the last time he'd seen her. Long blond hair, beautiful porcelain skin. Soft blue eyes. Only instead of smiling at the camera, her eyes were focused on the infant she held in her arms.

"That was taken fifteen years ago this past April." The girl turned the phone back and looked at the image, that same smile—Missy's smile—on her face. "I was only a couple of weeks old at the time."

Fifteen years ago.

The months and years rushed through his head, the numbers making his brain go into a serious meltdown. The imaginary rein he'd been holding onto slipped from his grip, the wild beast beneath him disappeared and he was flying through the air.

"Missy…" he rasped, determined to push the words past the restricted confines of his dry throat. "Missy Ellington is your mother?"

"Abso-bloody-lutely." The girl's gaze was serious as she looked up at him again. "And you're my father."

* * *

Blimey, he still looked good.

After sixteen years, Missy Dobbs had thought he would have changed, but no, Liam Murphy had only grown more handsome than the boy who'd stolen her heart all those years ago.

She pulled in a deep breath. She had to do this. There was no gray area to fill with *could she* or *should she* when it came to this decision. The certainty of what lay ahead outweighed the fear, although not by much.

The hustle and bustle of the busy airport gate continued on around her as she waited for a flight that would take her to the last place on earth she'd ever thought she would see again.

Destiny, Wyoming.

She tightened her grip on the tablet as she stared again at Liam's picture on the website for his family's company. She tried to reconcile the wild and crazy cowboy she'd known as a teen with the serious man looking impossibly dashing in a business suit. The dark-framed glasses he wore couldn't hide the sparkle in his eyes and his hair was shorter now, but a wayward curl or two still threatened to spill down over his forehead.

Her former love had done well for himself. CEO and president of his family's business. She wasn't surprised. Liam had been cut out for more than being a rodeo star, but at eighteen that had been his dream.

A dream that had torn them apart.

A dream that had sent her running home and into a fateful one-night stand with a former boyfriend. A man she'd ended up marrying because she believed—she'd been told—he was the true father of her child after finding out she was pregnant a few months later. Only now—after many years, she knew the truth.

Liam Murphy was her daughter's father.

What a bloody mess!

She hadn't even talked to Casey about what she'd learned before heading to Los Angeles on a last-minute work assignment. No, there'd only been time for a heated argument with her mother, who'd known the truth about Casey's paternity all along.

That had been two weeks ago.

Her job on the film set had finished late yesterday and Casey was set to fly in on Monday to join Missy for an extended holiday here in the States. That meant Missy had the weekend to fly to Destiny, knock on Liam's door with the hope he remembered her and break the news to him that he'd fathered a child.

The gentle chiming of her mobile phone came from deep within her purse. She didn't recognize the number and offered a quick prayer that it wasn't anything work related that would cancel her plans.

"Hello?"

"Mum, it's me. Casey."

Missy slammed the tablet's cover closed, almost as if her daughter could see what she'd been looking at.

Other than texting back and forth, they hadn't talked in the last few days. And when they had chatted during Missy's stay in Los Angeles, she hadn't mentioned anything about what she'd discovered to her daughter. Sharing the news about Casey's real father had to wait until they were together again, face-to-face.

"Ah, hello, sweetie. Why aren't you calling me from your mobile?"

"It died. Completely. I've got it charging at the moment."

The airport's loudspeaker came to life, blaring out information. Missy turned to the wall and ducked her head in hopes of muffling the noise. She quickly figured the time difference between California and London. It was after dinnertime there. "Are you home now? You need to start packing."

"Not...exactly."

Two words—and the nervous hitch in her daughter's voice—sent a shiver of maternal alertness through Missy. "Laundry might be your least favorite chore for a Friday night, sweetie, but you can't wait until the last minute to figure out what to bring for our holiday—"

Her daughter's words cut her off midsentence. "Mum, I don't have to worry about packing because I'm already here."

Here? In Los Angeles?

Missy jerked to her feet, her leather tote swinging from her shoulder. She scanned the gate area for an airport map. "What do you mean, *here*? Are you at the LAX international terminal?"

"No, I'm in Wyoming."

What?

Missy's precarious hold on a reality that had been spinning out of control over the last few weeks slipped away. She dropped to the unyielding airport seat beneath her, the ability to stand gone as the blood drained from her head.

"Mum? Did you hear me?" Casey asked. "Mum?"

"How did—why are—" Missy pushed the words past her lips, unable to complete either question. She finally managed to squeak out, "Why on earth would you fly to Wyoming? Alone?"

"I was planning to fly to LA alone, wasn't I? Blimey, it's not like it's the first time I've traveled by myself."

Yes, Casey had started joining her at film locations during school breaks a few years ago, but those were always nonstop flights around Europe.

"Of course, but again, why—" Missy's heart pounded in her chest, the truth already settling like a rock in her belly. "Why are you in—"

"Why do you think? I overheard bits and bobs when you and Grandmum fought the night before you flew to California. About what you found in Granddad's desk. I can't believe they did that to you! To us!" Her daughter's words came fast. "And you didn't talk to me before your flight or the few times we've chatted since. Not one word!"

Oh, this was not how she wanted this to go. "Sweetie, I—"

"Not that I blame you, really. I mean, it's not exactly a topic for casual conversation," Casey barreled on. "I heard you say a man's name and a town in Wyoming during your argument, so after some online searching I decided to change my flight plans. I arrived in Cheyenne this morning."

Missy tried to keep up, but her daughter's words blended with the loud rushing in her ears and the announcement that her flight was boarding. She gathered her items and got in line, the boarding pass shaking in a mad fit in her fingers.

Casey was in Wyoming. She knew about Liam.

Fix this! Fix this! Fix this!

The words thundered inside Missy's brain as she made her way to her first-class seat, trying to think of what to say—what to do—next.

Casey could wait for her at the airport. They'd get a hotel room and talk. She'd figure out a way to get in touch with Liam tomorrow.

Slightly calmer after her hastily thought up plan, Missy said, "Okay, I want you to stay at the airport. I'm on a flight—"

"Mum, I'm not in Cheyenne anymore. I'm in Destiny!

And guess what?" Casey's voice rose in excitement before it dropped to a loud whisper. "I found him."

Destiny! Missy's impetuous daughter had traveled from London to a small ranching community in the American West and found the man who was her true father.

Missy dropped into her seat, staring numbly at the seat in front of her.

"Mum? Are you still there? Mum?"

She needed to answer her daughter, needed to know what had happened in the last twenty-four hours. Needed to know how Liam had reacted to the bombshell her—their—daughter had dropped at his feet today. But there wasn't time. She would have to end this call soon and Casey still didn't know Missy was making her way to Wyoming.

Pulling in a deep breath through her nose, she released it in a soft wisp past her lips. By the third one she was able to speak. "Honey, we need to talk."

"I couldn't agree more."

Missy gasped. The same deep, gravelly, sexy voice she remembered from her youth filled her ear and stole her breath. A heated flush that made no sense at all started in the center of her chest and rushed to every part of her body.

How could he sound exactly the same after all this time? "Liam."

She heard a swift intake of breath, and then silence filled the distance—both in miles and years—that stretched between them.

Up until the last few weeks, she hadn't spoken his name aloud in a long time. Not when she and her girlfriends would gather for drinks and a chat, not to her daughter when they talked about things like boys and dating and growing up, and never to her parents.

Sometimes it felt as if that year in her life had happened to someone else.

"Casey tells me you've been in Los Angeles for the last few weeks." Liam's voice was clipped and businesslike now. "If you let me know where you're staying, I'll make arrangements to get you to the airport and on a flight to Wyoming right away."

Bristling at his authoritative tone, she said, "I'm on a flight to Cheyenne scheduled to depart in a few minutes, actually. I land at half past five, local time."

There was more silence as he processed her news. Was he surprised she'd already been on her way? How much had her daughter told him about the night Missy—and she—had learned the truth?

"I'll be there when your plane lands," he finally said.

Of course he would. And since she hadn't thought far enough ahead to figure out how she would travel to Destiny, she wouldn't fight him. Getting to Casey was the most important thing at the moment. "May I speak to my daughter again?"

His voice dropped away, and then Casey's voice came back on the line. "You're flying here? Like right now?"

"Yes, sweetie, and I promise we'll talk about everything when I see you." Missy tried to keep her voice light. "Including you changing your transatlantic flight. Please don't cause any trouble for…for Liam in the meanwhile."

"You're a tad late for that bit of advice, Mum." Casey offered a staged sigh, an expression the teen had perfected in the last few years. "I'd say me showing up out of the blue is just the start of trouble."

Missy popped a breath mint into her mouth and made stopping by the loo her first priority as soon as she landed in Cheyenne.

After using the facilities and washing her hands, she redid her hair, making neat the messy chignon style she favored. When she found herself leaning toward the mirror to reapply her lipstick, she froze.

Did she care what Liam Murphy thought of her after all this time?

Not wanting to answer that question, she hurried to the baggage claim area and found her case still circling the carousel. She retrieved it and then checked her phone. No calls or texts from her daughter or Liam. With a thirty-minute stopover in Denver, she'd only had time to ring her mother and have their first real conversation since Missy had left London.

Wise enough to keep her opinions of Casey's actions to herself, her mother had insisted she had no idea what her granddaughter had been up to. But Elizabeth Ellington had been shocked to find out Missy was also on her way to Wyoming. Before she could say anything more, Missy had ended the call with a curt promise to get in touch as soon as she found a place for her and Casey to stay for the weekend.

"Ms. Dobbs?"

Missy spun around and found a gentleman dressed in a dark suit holding a placard with her name on it. She'd traveled enough over the years to recognize a car service when she saw one.

Liam wasn't here. She should be grateful for more time before she saw him again, but it bothered her more than she cared to admit that he hadn't kept his word. "Yes?"

"Mr. Murphy was unavoidably detained in Destiny due to business," he said. "I'm to make sure you arrive safely. I have a car waiting outside."

Resentment burned that not only had Liam stood her up, but he hadn't sent Casey along to meet her either. Bollocks! What did he think she'd do? Grab her daughter and take the next flight out of here?

"Could you give me a moment, please?" she asked.

The gentleman nodded and stepped away. Missy found a quiet corner and called Casey's mobile. It went straight to voice mail. She left a message that she'd landed and was on her way to Destiny. She then tried the number her daughter had used when she'd called earlier today, assuming it was for Liam's cell phone, but it just rang and rang.

Seeing as she didn't have any other choice, she followed the driver outside and moments later was seated in the back of a luxury town car. They soon were out of the city and on the motorway. Out the window the land was flat and wide and empty with a blue sky that seemed to go on forever.

So different from the hustle and bustle of London, where she'd lived all her life. She remembered feeling very lost and vulnerable when she'd first arrived in Wyoming all those years ago.

She'd almost cut her visit short after a trip home for Christmas, but had decided to return to Destiny.

Because of one boy. The one she'd been crushing on from the time she'd seen him in the school hallway the very first week.

Liam Murphy, a real cowboy who spent his weekends riding in rodeos, had finally asked her to dance during the last slow song at the winter semiformal, and she had promptly tripped over his boots—

No!

Missy gave her head a quick shake. There would be no trips down memory lane. It was bad enough she'd spent the last few weeks remembering how she and Liam had met, started dating and fallen in love.

Of course, steering clear of their shared history wasn't going to be easy. Goodness knew what kind of questions Casey was going to have for her—for them—over the next few days.

Missy tried once more to reach her daughter, but again she got only voice mail. She grew more nervous as they arrived in Destiny, which she had to admit looked much the same as the last time she was here.

They drove down the charming main street with its many businesses, around the gazebo in the center of town, past the firehouse and the sheriff's office and the Blue Creek Saloon, a bar and restaurant whose roots went back to the town's founding in the late 1800s, a fact that had fascinated Missy the first time she'd been there.

When the car passed over the rushing waters of the blue creek the town landmark was named after, she realized the turnoff to Liam's family ranch and business headquarters was just ahead.

She tensed, expecting a large crowd. Liam was one of six boys, most of whom worked for the log-home business as well, so there must be wives and other children in the family by now. Would they be here? What about his parents? Were they still alive and living here, too?

When the car bypassed the oversize parking lot and slowed to a stop in the half circle drive in front of the massive two-story log home, only one figure waited on the front porch that ran the length of the building.

Liam.

From her own memories and the candid photographs on the company's website showing the Murphy family at work and at play, the brothers were all good-looking men with similar features, but she knew it was him.

Missy couldn't take her eyes off the man as she exited the car and pushed her tote bag to one shoulder, her fingers clenching her phone as the memories she'd tried so hard to keep at bay washed over her.

Memories of falling in love for the first time, and all the joy and wonder that came with that experience. But then the pain—a truly aching, physical pain—when he had broken her heart.

How, after all this time, could those feelings still be powerful enough to bring a piercing sting to the back of her eyes?

Blinking hard, she wished she'd thought to grab her sunglasses from her bag. Regardless, she started forward, suddenly needing to see Casey. She made her way up the elaborate brick pathway, bordered with a colorful array of flowers that also ran along the front of the house.

"Where's my daughter?" she asked when she reached the stairs, hating the huskiness of her voice.

Liam moved to the edge of the porch and she couldn't help but note that the picture online must've been taken recently. Despite the passage of time, he did look the same, just an older version of the boy she'd known. Impossibly handsome in jeans, a long-sleeved dress shirt with the cuffs folded back to his elbows and cowboy boots.

Always cowboy boots.

His gaze lit on her, but the setting sun and deep shadows of the porch made it impossible to see his expression as he thanked the driver, who'd placed her suitcases on the porch. She tore her gaze from him and thanked the man as well when he walked past her.

When it was just the two of them again, she returned her focus to Liam, who hadn't moved other than to cross his arms over his chest.

The defensive pose spoke volumes about his state of mind. Fine, but right now she wanted to see for herself that Casey was okay.

"I asked you—"

"Is it true?" The words were out of his mouth as she reached for the stair railing, freezing her on the first step. "Is Casey my daughter?" he demanded.

Chapter Two

Liam hadn't meant to sound so rude. He'd figured once Missy arrived at the house they'd sit down like adults, catch up on the last sixteen years and talk about the craziness that had descended on his life today.

Craziness in the form of his supposed daughter. But first, he had to know.

"Is she mine?" he asked again, his voice softer now.

He waited for her to answer, not having felt this rush of fear, excitement and adrenaline since his bronc-riding days. No, that was a lie. The moment Casey had shocked him with her announcement, he'd felt something far beyond anything he'd ever experienced on the back of a horse.

The sensation now returned in full force. The feeling that he was about to take the ride of his life.

"Yes," Missy finally said, "she is."

He dropped his arms. The almost desperate need to

believe her was so foreign he brushed it away. Could he accept what she was saying as the truth? He'd admit the numbers made sense and according to his mother, Casey shared the same eyes—right down to the dark blue coloring—as him, but he was having a hard time believing the girl's rambling story.

None of this made sense. How? Why?

"I'd like to see her," Missy continued, her lilting voice laced with a condescending tone. "Now. If that's all right with you."

"You can't."

Realizing again how bad mannered that sounded, Liam tried once more to soften his tone. "She's at the rodeo with her gran—with my folks. My family. She had a good time today and didn't want to miss the finals, presentations to the winners or the fireworks afterward."

"Hmm, yes, I remember well how a rodeo works." Missy's smile was rueful as she continued up the steps toward him. "How can a mother compete with all that?"

She remembered because of him. Because of their time together. That thought caused a burst of heat to ignite right in the center of his chest.

"They also figured you and I would appreciate the opportunity to talk privately about…well, about everything."

"Saying we have quite a bit to discuss seems a bit of an understatement, doesn't it?"

Liam stepped back when she joined him on the porch but not before a summery floral scent with a hint of peach invaded his head. Damn, she still wore the same perfume. Swallowing hard against the rush of memories, he took a step back and gestured toward a seating area set up at the far end of the porch.

She moved past him, walking in that same graceful way she'd had as a teenager. Years of ballet training, she'd once told him. Her hair was the same honey-blond color, but she wore it up off her neck, a few long pieces curling around her face. He wondered if it was as long as it'd once been, halfway down her back.

As if she could read his mind, Missy paused when she reached the wicker sofa, one hand tucking back a strand of hair that had fallen free as her chin rose in an almost regal attitude before she sat.

Yeah, she still possessed that British reserve that had made it hard for her to make friends when she first came to Destiny all those years ago.

He'd noticed her the first day of his senior year in high school. Every guy had. She'd been so different from the rest of the girls in their class. Some of his friends had made fools of themselves, trying to capture her attention, but the more they tried, the more she shot them down.

As someone who never had any problem getting a pretty girl to notice him, he'd liked that about her.

After a few months of watching her, he'd been determined to melt that icy reserve—and brave enough to try thanks to a dare from his buddies at the winter semiformal.

It'd taken until the night was almost over before he asked her to dance. She'd surprised him by accepting, and like a klutz, he'd tangled his boots with her delicate shoes. She'd laughed it off, stepped into his arms and he'd been a goner.

"You're staring at me."

Her words—the same ones spoken by her daughter earlier today—had him shaking off the memories as he joined her, taking one of the chairs. "I'm sorry. After all these years…to see you again. I guess I'm comparing the photos Casey showed me to the real thing."

Missy rolled her eyes. "Her and that mobile. I think she must have five hundred pictures on it."

"Many of them are of the two of you. Some going back years."

She nodded, a soft smile on her face, and then her gaze met his again. "You look just like your photo, too."

It took him a moment to figure out where she might have seen a picture of him. Online. Thanks to their office manager's insistence, the company's site had been updated this summer with new pictures, including formal portraits of the management team.

Liam liked that she had done a Google search on him. "You visited the Murphy Mountain Log Homes website."

"Very corporate looking." Her gaze traveled over him. "You look good in Hugo Boss."

"They cut a good suit."

Silence stretched between them as they studied each other in the fading light of the sunset. Was she looking for the cowboy he'd been back then? Wild and reckless and so full of himself he couldn't see beyond his own wants and needs? His own dreams?

She looked exactly the same. Older, yes, but still the same ethereal beauty as when he'd last seen her. It was easy to see the features she shared with her daughter.

Their daughter.

His throat suddenly dry, Liam rose and went to the antique dresser that held pitchers of tea, water, an ice bucket and glasses, all thanks to his mother. "I'm sorry, I should've asked. Would you like something to drink?"

Missy let loose with a delicate humph from behind him. "Do you have anything a wee bit stronger? I think you're going to need it."

He shot her a look over his shoulder, and then opened the door below and pulled out a bottle of wine and his drink of choice, whiskey. She gestured for the wine and he poured her a glass, then whiskey for himself.

"You know, Casey tried to explain how she'd only found out a few weeks ago about me being her..." His voice trailed off as he returned to his seat, handing Missy her wine. "The more she talked, the more upset she became. I gather from your shock at her announcing she'd traveled to Destiny and found me that you hadn't shared this news with her yet?"

Missy placed her cell phone on the table and took the glass. "No, I didn't have the chance before my job had me flying to Los Angeles. I've barely had time to absorb everything myself. After all these years...to think, it never occurred to me to question the test results—"

It was at that moment his cell phone chirped from inside his pants pocket, cutting her off. Damn, now was not the time for business. He ignored the phone and it went silent for a moment, but came back to life again right away.

"You can get that," she said. "If you need to."

He probably should. A typical day for him ran long past five o'clock, especially for a select few clients who had his direct line. Or was it someone from the rodeo committee looking for him, despite his hasty explanation about a business emergency?

"It might be Casey," he said, the thought just coming to him.

Missy flipped over her phone, checking it. "I tried to ring her when I landed. All I got was voice mail."

He pulled the now silent phone out and looked. Two missed calls, both from the same client, who wouldn't hesitate to move on to his brother Nolan if he couldn't reach Liam. A press of a button and the phone would stay quiet.

"It was work, but it can wait," he said. "Now, you were saying something about test results? Casey mentioned overhearing a fight between you and her grandmother, but like I said, she was pretty distraught. I told her we'd get everything straightened out when you got here. After that, she seemed to relax and enjoy the rodeo."

"And you introduced her to your family?" Missy sipped her wine. "Just like that?"

"I wasn't about to leave her on her own to wander around the fairgrounds. I told them she was the daughter of an old friend from high school." He took a swallow from his own glass, the familiar warmth sliding easily down his throat. "As soon as I said your name my folks remembered you. So did my younger brother Bryant. It was my mom who...well, who put it all together, especially when I said you were on your way to Destiny."

"And here I am."

"Yes, here you are." And here he was waiting for his first love to explain how he—they—had a child he'd never known about until today. "After all this time, not hearing from you, I can honestly say I never expected something like...this."

"I can understand. Please, let me start at the beginning. Well, the most recent beginning." She sighed, her gaze lowered. "My father passed away suddenly from a heart attack on August first."

"I'm sorry," Liam said automatically, surprised at how little emotion was in her voice considering that was just three weeks ago. "Was he ill?"

"Thank you, and technically he wasn't, but it was his third attack in the last ten years. Not completely unexpected, especially as he refused to give up his cigars and brandy." She paused and pulled in a deep breath. "I was going through his desk after the services, clearing out paperwork and whatnot, when I came across a file that contained the DNA test we had done just after Casey was born."

"April twelfth, a week after your birthday."

She looked up when he said that. "Yes."

"She told me. That was nine months after we'd last— after you returned home."

"Yes."

"Almost nine months to the day, if memory serves."

"Yes."

"Missy, why didn't you tell me?" Tired of her one-word answers, Liam leaned forward, bracing his forearms against his knees, his fingers laced tight around the glass. "I know things ended badly, but as soon as you knew you were pregnant you should've gotten in touch with me."

"I wanted to, but I didn't… I didn't know if I had the right to."

"The right?" Now he was really confused. "What does that mean?"

"Oh, Liam, I was such a mess when I left Destiny all those years ago." She set her glass on the table, stood and then walked to the porch railing, keeping her back to him. "You and I had that terrible row. All my plans and dreams were gone. I was angry and lonely and…"

"And?" He prompted when her voice faded.

Her shoulders rose and fell as she pulled in another deep breath before turning to face him, her arms tight across her middle. "And I spent the night with my old boyfriend. The lad I was seeing before I came to America. Before you."

The fine Kentucky whiskey now burned in his gut. "Stanley." The name popped out of his mouth before he could think to stop it.

"Stanford. His name was Stanford Dobbs."

He vaguely remembered her telling him all those years ago about a college guy she'd been dating back in London. Hearing his full name—with the same surname as Missy and Casey—had him taking another long swallow of liquid courage. "And this happened soon after you got back that summer?"

She jerked her head in a quick nod, the affirmation tearing at his insides. How crazy was that?

"The following week," she said softly. "It…it was only that one time. After that, I knew I had to pull myself together, get my life back on track. Get back into school. Get over you."

To hear her speak calmly about sleeping with someone else so soon after they—after she returned, despite all the time that had passed, bugged Liam more than he wanted to admit.

Leaning back in his chair, he offered her a casual salute with his glass, his knuckles white. "Well, that was a step in the right direction."

She bit hard at her bottom lip, and then continued. "I didn't realize I was pregnant until almost Halloween."

Now it all made sense. "And you didn't know who the father was."

"No, I didn't." She returned his stare, unflinching. "It took me another month to find the courage to tell Stanford…and my parents. They, of course, expected a hasty wedding, but when I told them that there was no way to be sure—"

"Boy, that must've made Stan a bit upset."

Up went that delicate chin again. "Stanford still wanted to marry me. He said he didn't care if the child was his or not."

Okay, Liam should feel like a louse right about now, but the fire burning in his gut had now spread throughout his body. "That was big of him."

"We had to wait until Casey was born before a DNA test could be done. Before we knew for certain who was—"

"But you *knew* you were pregnant the previous fall."

Liam shot to his feet. "You knew there was a chance—why didn't you at least let me know that the baby might be mine?"

"Oh, Liam, you were on the other side of the world, living your dream. You'd made your decision to be a professional cowboy that summer, and you continued right on with your rodeo competitions after I left. By the time I knew I was pregnant, you were well on your way to earning a spot at grand finals, finishing second your first time there!"

She knew that?

She must've read the shock on his face. "Yes, I knew, thanks to Suzy McIntyre. The girl whose family I stayed with while I was here in Destiny? She told me all about your big achievement in a letter that arrived just after the new year."

"Wait—you got a letter?" The memory returned so strong he dropped back to the chair. "From Suzy?"

"Believe me, no one was more surprised than I to see it in the post."

"That was the only letter you got?"

"Oh, one was more than enough." Missy's voice rose as she paced back and forth in front of him. "Not only did she send me a newspaper clipping of you being a rodeo star, but she also went on about how you and your *bride* were settling in here in Destiny afterward."

Liam closed his eyes and swallowed hard. He hadn't thought about that stupid and reckless decision in a long time. "She told you I had gotten married?"

"Yes! Six months after I left."

The pain in Missy's voice surprised him. He looked at her again. "It didn't last. Six or seven— it was over by the spring."

"Well, I didn't want to upset the newlyweds unless I

had to, so I waited until my daughter was born that same spring." Missy returned to the seating area and grabbed her glass. "When the test results came back that Stanford was a match...we married a month later."

The only sound was the low chirping of crickets now that the sun had set. And there was a distant thunder that could only be the fireworks from the rodeo. It was then that Liam noticed the outside lights on the porch, pathway and the model homes situated in front of the main house had come on automatically, casting muted pockets of yellow glowing here and there, but the end of the porch where they sat was dark.

So dark that he couldn't see Missy's face clearly.

He rose again. Lighting candles on the dresser, he brought back a few and placed them in the center of the table in time to catch the shaking of the glass in her hand.

"I was nineteen years old, a mother, a wife...trying to go to school, to live up to my parents' expectations...to Stanford's." Missy finished the last of her wine. "It wasn't easy."

He was sure it wasn't. At nineteen he'd been concentrating on rodeoing full-time and working for his father, attached to nothing but his horse and trailer. Not even his so-called marriage had rated any importance. One of the reasons it'd ended so quickly.

How long had Missy and Stanford been married? Were they still?

Liam's gaze went to her left hand clutching the glass. No ring. Did that mean anything? "Casey never mentioned her father today."

"Stanford died in a car accident when she was five years old. Before that we were—he traveled a lot. For business. She barely remembers him."

So, she hadn't remarried in the decade since? He tucked

away that question, not wanting to go there. "You started to tell me about test results. I'm guessing you're referring to the ones that said Stanford was a match."

"Yes, but what I found in the dark corners of my father's desk were two test results," Missy said, reaching for an oversize leather tote. She tilted it toward the light and rummaged around inside, pulling out some paperwork and thrusting it at him. "The one he showed me all those years ago and the *real* test. The one that stated Stanford was not a match. This, of course, meant you were—are—Casey's father."

Liam took the papers, but kept his eyes on her. "I'm guessing this is what you and your mother argued about."

"You bet your arse. She admitted to knowing the whole thing, all this time, when I confronted her." Missy grabbed her glass, saw it was empty and set it down again. "Like I said, I had to fly to LA the next day for a work commitment without the chance to talk to Casey. I couldn't have sprung something like this on her at the last minute and then left. Not that it mattered. Apparently she overheard me and Mum and…and took matters into her own hands."

She looked at him then, her gaze steady. "The one thing I did plan was coming to Destiny. To find you and tell you everything. Casey got here first."

Liam nodded, certain if he tried to speak right now the words wouldn't make it past the lump in his throat.

He tried to mentally piece together the jigsaw puzzle her story created. He believed her, as crazy as it was. He was angry at her parents for what they had done to both of them—all three of them. To keep the true paternity of their grandchild from their daughter because…

He had no idea why. Other than that they must've been dead set against the plans Missy had made all those years ago to move to America. To go to college here. To be with him. Plans he'd stomped all over with his size-twelve boots when he'd announced *his* plan to rodeo full-time instead of going to the University of Wyoming.

So where did they go from here?

"I planned to tell Casey once we were together again. She wasn't supposed to arrive in the States until Monday, meeting me in LA," Missy continued. "She, of course, took it upon herself to change all that."

"Who was watching Casey while you traveled? Your mother?"

Missy nodded.

"I'm guessing she too was in the dark about Casey's plans." Liam leaned forward and set his now empty glass down. "Does she know where her granddaughter is now?"

"Of course. We spoke during my layover. And yes, she had no idea what Casey was up to. She was under the impression she was staying with friends."

"You seem pretty calm about all of this—"

She cut him off with a casual wave of her hand. "Believe me, I'm not."

"Really?" There was that cool British reserve again, and it irked him. "Your daughter changes her international flight plans, arrives alone in a foreign country and hitches a ride to Destiny from the airport and you're just—"

Her beautiful blue eyes grew wide. "Hitched?"

"It was just pure luck that I ran into her at the rodeo at all. In time to get her out of what might've been a... sticky situation."

"I'm not sure what that means, but believe me, I will be discussing my daughter's actions with her as soon as I see her." Missy dropped her hand to the tote in her lap. "And answering what I'm sure will be quite a few questions from her about this entire situation. Thankfully, she and I have plenty of time to talk. We're flying to Hawaii next week for a planned holiday before returning to London next month."

Liam's head spun, his thoughts a jumbled mess of questions, ideas and plans, but her words cut through. "Wait a minute, you mean you *were* flying to Hawaii."

"No, I—"

"Don't think you can just show up, drop a bomb about a long-lost daughter and walk away three days later." Liam's anger was back and it was hot. He got to his feet again. "I don't care who got here first."

"We have plans."

"Plans change."

She stood as well, ready to argue, but then a caravan of cars came down the drive. They parked in the nearby lot and his family spilled out into the night. Moments later they were across the yard and heading up the porch, with Casey leading the way.

"Mum!"

Missy's expression transformed when she saw her daughter, and seconds later they held each other in a tight embrace. When they finally let go, Missy stepped back, running her hands lightly over Casey's multicolored hair as she looked in her daughter's eyes. Then she took in the new boots Casey was proudly showing off.

Watching the two of them, and the private world they created just by being in each other's company, made Liam's chest ache. This was supposed to be his daughter, but he'd never felt more like an outsider despite being surrounded by his own family.

He cleared his throat, catching both of their attention.

"Missy, I think you probably remember my folks, Alistair and Elise Murphy." The sooner they got introductions over with, the sooner they could get back to talking about how long she and Casey were sticking around. "Mom and Dad, this is Casey's mother, Melissa Dobbs."

She took his mother's outstretched hand first and then his father's. "Yes, of course, I remember you, Mr. and Mrs. Murphy. It's good to see you again. And please, call me Missy."

"Oh, it's so nice to see you, too, dear," his mother said, giving her the once-over before sending a wink Liam's way that he hoped no one else noticed. "We remember you as well. You've grown up so nice."

"Ah, thank you."

"And these are two of my three brothers who live in town." Liam waved at the men standing nearby. "I'm guessing Adam took Fay and A.J. straight on home?"

"Only because the baby was fussy. Otherwise they would've been here too. Hi, Missy, I'm Nolan Murphy." Liam's brother stepped forward and gave her a quick handshake. "Adam's our oldest brother and the smart one. He doesn't live here on the compound." He then pointed at the three teenagers lounging on the steps. "Those hooligans are mine. Abby is sixteen and the twins, Luke and Logan, are thirteen."

Missy smiled at the kids and then returned his greeting. "I'm sorry, I don't remember meeting you before. Or Adam."

"That's because I was living in Boston the year you were here. Adam was serving overseas in the military."

After nodding, she then shook hands with Bryant and his wife, Laurie. "Now, you I remember," she said. "You were a wee freshman when I was here last."

"Yeah, that was me." Bryant grinned. "Devlin is only a year behind Liam, so you must remember him too."

"Yes, I do remember Devlin. Popular with the ladies, right?"

"Oh, that's our Dev," Elise said, and then laughed. "Only now he's a one-woman man and living in London, actually, for the next few months, with his lady love, Tanya. And our youngest, Ric—oh, he must've been just six or seven when you were here—is in the air force, stationed in northern Italy."

"Well, it's lovely to meet you all…again…and thank you for taking care of my daughter today. I do appreciate it."

"We enjoyed having her with us." Elise smiled warmly at Casey, waving off Missy's gratitude. "And we're looking forward to getting to know her—and you—better during your stay."

Missy glanced at her daughter for a moment before her gaze flickered in Liam's direction. "Well, we're only in town for a few days," she said, looking back at his mother. "The weekend. Casey and I have a holiday scheduled—"

"Mum, are you daft? We can't go now!" Casey spun around, grabbing her arm. "I just got here. We just got here! There's so much more I want to see and do!"

"Casey, we have reservations—"

"Off the bloody reservations! Everything's changed now!"

Liam couldn't agree more, but from the look on Missy's face, she wasn't buying into her daughter's excitement.

"Why don't we head inside and let these three talk this out," Alistair said, heading for the door with his wife in tow.

"Are you kidding?" Abby leaned in from her perch on the stairs, flinging her long blond hair back over one shoulder. "This is getting good!"

"Nolan…"

Liam sent his brother a warning look, but the man was already corralling his kids off the steps and around the side yard. Bryant and Laurie followed his folks indoors. Then it was the three of them as Casey continued her campaign to change her mother's mind.

It wasn't working.

He could see it in Missy's eyes, hear it in her voice as she laid out the travel plans she and Casey had for spending the next month in a private villa on the beach in Maui. Nice. She'd come from a world of money and power back when they'd first met all those years ago. He guessed she—or her family—was still doing okay.

Either way, she didn't want to be in Destiny. Didn't want to be near him. Too bad. If she thought she could waltz out of the continental US, taking his daughter with her, and expect him to be okay with that, she had another think coming.

His fingers tightened into a fist, crinkling the paperwork he still held. An idea popped into his head and tumbled out of his mouth. "Here's another reason for you two to stick around. We need to do another DNA test."

The two women stopped talking and turned in unison to look at him.

Missy's light blue eyes crackled with fire, but it was the wounded look that flashed in Casey's that got to him.

Damn, what else could he do?

He believed Missy's story about a doctored DNA test, even if it was a bit farfetched. Who knew how long this lie would've gone on if not for her father suddenly dying, Casey overhearing, Liam still living in the same town where it all started…

For whatever reason, the universe had conspired to bring him and Missy back together—to bring them all together—and he wanted them to stay. More than he'd wanted anything in a long time.

"Look, this is a negative report telling us who's not a match," Liam said, gesturing with the paperwork. "A report we now know that has been tampered with. We should have another test done—me and Casey—just so we're all a hundred percent sure."

Chapter Three

Casey was ready to tell her real father what he could do with his suggestion about a new DNA test, and knowing her daughter's temper, it wasn't going to be pretty. Not that Missy blamed her. After his veiled remarks concerning her parenting skills, she was ready to tell him what he could do with his demand for another test herself.

"I think he's right," she said instead, before Casey could speak. She read the surprise on Liam's face at her like-mindedness, but her focus at the moment had to be on her daughter.

Missy reached for Casey's hand, hating that it was ice-cold. A quick squeeze got her attention. "We should have an up-to-date test done. For his sake, sweetie, and ours."

Casey's bravado crumbled and the fire left her eyes. "Why did Granddad do this to you? To us? To Dad?" She bit hard at her bottom lip, and her gaze swung over to Liam. "I mean…you know, my other…"

"It's okay." Liam's voice was gentler now. "Things are a little mixed-up at the moment."

To say the least. The hurt and confusion reflected on Liam's and Casey's faces—feelings that shone brightly in matching sets of dark blue eyes—shook Missy to her core.

Almost as much as the realization that the two of them shared the same eyes. Same shape, same color. A deep cerulean blue she'd once told Liam matched the river-fed lake back behind the Murphy family home. A color she always told Casey was her favorite.

How had she never noticed that before now?

Because you believed the lie you were told years ago. The scared girl deep inside you clung to those test results, filled with righteous indignation that this man didn't deserve to be the father of your precious baby girl.

Missy blinked away that sudden insight, not willing or able to deal with that bitter pill of truth. Not tonight. "I think we should—"

"How did you two hook up anyway?" Casey blurted out. "It's a long way between London and Destiny—oh, wait! I overheard Grandmum say letting you go to America was a mistake. You'd turned nineteen just before you had me... bollocks, don't tell me I'm a souvenir from a one-off during a spring break trip."

"No!" Liam and Missy spoke at the same time, their voices united.

"You were not the result of a one-night stand," Missy continued, aghast that the idea had popped into her daughter's head.

"You never told her?" he asked, taking a step closer. His broad shoulders blocked out the porch light behind him, casting his face in shadows, but the tightening of his jaw was unmistakable. "About your time in Destiny? About us?"

Missy shook her head, surprised at the nuance of hurt in his tone. No, that was impossible. The man had married someone else less than a year after she'd left sixteen years ago. A lifetime ago.

"That's right. You said a few minutes ago you remembered his family!" Casey's voice grew excited again. "So you two were a couple? And you lived here in Destiny, Mum? For how long?"

"A year," Liam said.

"It was more like eleven months." Missy spoke at the same time, overriding him. "As part of a student exchange program when I was in my sixth form. The twelfth grade in an American high school, and yes, Liam and I dated during that time."

"I'd say you did more than date, Mum. A lot more."

Liam let loose a snort that changed to a clearing of his throat, one hand fisted against his mouth, when Missy glared at him. Still, he remained silent, only tilting his head in her direction.

She sighed. She wanted nothing more than to sink up to her nose in bubbles and then collapse into bed, but some private time with her daughter was needed first.

"Sweetie, it's been a long day. For all of us. Right now, I could use a hot bath and we—" she gave Casey's hand another quick squeeze "—need to have a long talk. About everything. Including your clandestine adventure getting to America, which, despite everything, you're not off the hook for."

Her daughter's gaze again flickered to Liam.

"A talk with just the two of us," Missy added, this time looking fully at Liam, half expecting him to argue with her over this as well. "If that's all right with you?"

He returned her stare for a long moment, and then nodded. "If you think that's best." He dropped his hand to his side. "For now."

Meaning Casey and he—or more likely the three of them—would be talking about their shared past, and where they all went from here, during the next few days. At least his anger about their planned holiday seemed to have disappeared, probably because of Casey's vocal objections to leaving Destiny.

Not that agreeing to another test meant anything had changed.

Still, things had gone better than Missy had hoped for tonight. Considering the merry-go-round of memories, emotions and questions that she'd been riding since that night in her father's study, Missy was proud of how she'd handled things so far.

Once she and her daughter started talking? All bets were off.

Casey had never been one to back down from what she was feeling, and like most teenagers, she could get a bit cheeky when her emotions were riled, not holding back whatever she might be thinking. Missy was used to it, even if she did have to pull in Casey's reins from time to time. The truth was she'd encouraged her daughter to always speak her mind and be honest with what she was feeling. A trait that often exasperated Casey's grandparents, especially her grandmother.

It was time to end this evening before she went into memory overload. "Liam, if you could arrange for a car to take us to the closest hotel, perhaps that quaint bed-and-breakfast in town, we'd greatly appreciate it."

Her heart stuttered when he gave a quick shake of his head. "No can do. The inn is full. So are the two hotels out by the highway. With the rodeo in town, there isn't an empty room anywhere. People are staying as far away as Laramie. Even Cheyenne."

"Well, we have to stay somewhere. I doubt we'll be able to do anything about a test until Monday." She released Casey and turned back for the phone she'd left on the table. "Let me do a search and see what I can find—"

"How about we stay here? Who's living in those?"

"Cassalyn Dobbs!" Missy spun back around, surprised by the boldness of her daughter, who was pointing at the nearby log homes. "How cheeky of you."

"She's not being *cheeky*, just curious." Liam again shook his head, this time with a slight smile on his face. "Sorry, but those are only model homes. They have electricity, as you can see, but no plumbing. Since your mother mentioned wanting a bubble bath—"

"I didn't say anything about bubbles," she cut him off, her gaze on her phone, positive she hadn't spoken that desire aloud. "And we can't stay here."

"Of course you can." Elise Murphy's voice carried from the doorway as she came back out to the porch. "You're more than welcome."

Stay here in the Murphy family home? Not bloody likely!

Now it was Missy's turn to shake her head. "Oh, we wouldn't want to impose—"

"It's no imposition, dear." Elise hurried to join them. "We'd love to have you. Now, we do have an empty guest room in the main house, but it only has a queen-size bed. Much too small for the two of you. Nolan's place is out— what with the four of them, it's already crowded and why he turned his guest room into an office I'll never understand."

"He likes to work late," Liam said. "Really late."

"And he can't walk across the yard to his office here in the main house?" Elise harrumphed. "Bryant and Laurie's

cabin is too small. And you—" she paused to swat at her
son's chest "—if you'd bother to furnish any of the rooms
in your new place beside the master suite—"

"My place has furniture," Liam interrupted his mother.
"Just not in the bedrooms."

"And aren't you sorry about that now?"

The flash of awareness in his gaze caused Missy's already hastened heartbeat to race out of control. Pressing
a hand to her chest, as if that would ease the wild thump-
ing, she tried to put a stop to this. "I appreciate your offer,
but we'll be fine in a hotel."

"Wait, I have the perfect place!" The older woman's
eyes lit up as she clasped her hands together. "You can
stay in the boathouse."

"The boathouse?" Casey asked. "What's that?"

"It's down back, on the lake. Above where we store the
boats and canoes and stuff. It used to be a storage area, but
a few years ago I came up with the idea of…"

Missy's gaze locked with Liam's, his mother's chatter
fading to a dull buzzing. The boathouse. A private sanctuary in the middle of the Murphy family madness she
and Liam had often sneaked off to whenever they wanted
to be alone.

They'd discovered the secluded setting by accident one
cool and stormy spring afternoon after hurrying back from
a canoe ride, soaked to the skin and looking for shelter.

Filled with cast-off furniture, old toys and boxes and
trunks filled with everything from books to clothes to holiday decorations, the place had had a faint musty smell, but
it'd been warm and dry. After realizing no one had found
out where they'd gone off to, they'd returned often. Just
being together, away from everyone, had been wonderful.

Of course, the intimacy of the space had lent itself to
kisses…and so much more. It'd been the first place they'd

made love. On a warm night with moonlight streaming through the windows, both unsure of what they were doing, but secure in their feelings and what they wanted.

A wanting that deepened and grew—

"Missy?"

Liam's husky voice broke into her memories, but it was his heated touch on her arm that jolted her out of the past.

She jerked away, refusing to look at him or accept the wild beating of her heart. Thankfully Elise was still going on about the design of the apartment, and her daughter was so enthralled with the description neither one of them had noticed how she had zoned out.

Liam had. Of course he had. He knew exactly why she was about to refuse his mother's generous offer.

"Us dropping in unannounced like this isn't fair to Liam…or to your family." Missy prayed her words didn't sound as distressed as she felt. "We really don't want to put you to any trouble."

"Oh, it's no trouble, dear. We were expecting a visit from friends of Alistair's for the rodeo, but they had to cancel at the last minute. The place is ready with fresh linens and a fully stocked kitchen."

"It sounds perfect." Casey offered a pleading look. "Please, Mum?"

It was late and the constant memories were draining, both emotionally and physically. Besides, after all this time, what did it really matter?

Hating the lump of desperation in her stomach at that thought, she forced a smile. "Thank you. We appreciate your hospitality."

Elise smiled and handed a key ring to her son. "Here, perhaps you should take them around through the backyard. There's still a group of people in the living room. We'll see you both in the morning."

His mother gave Casey a quick hug, which her daughter easily returned, surprising Missy again. She'd be hard-pressed to remember the last time she saw *her* mother exchange affections that way with Casey.

After the woman went back inside, the teen hurried to the stairs, grabbing Missy's two small suitcases along with a duffel bag she recognized as belonging to her daughter.

"Blimey, Mum...only two cases? I thought you took a whole store full when you departed for California."

"Most of which is still in LA," she quipped, joining her daughter after getting her purse. "I only brought enough clothes for a weekend trip."

"But we aren't—"

She lightly tugged at her earlobe—a familiar gesture between them that had the desired effect of stopping Casey from arguing. For the moment, at least. Her daughter's expression said she was clearly gearing up for round two.

Oh, a tub full of bubbles was sounding better all the time.

"Here, you take the key and let me carry those." Liam relieved Casey of the luggage and gestured for them to head down the stairs first. "Let's get you two settled. Casey, you know the way."

As she followed her daughter, Missy wondered what Liam meant by that last statement.

"We came home earlier for dinner," Liam said, falling into step beside her as they strolled down the lighted stone path that led around the side of the house. "Dad barbecued and then everyone headed back to the rodeo."

Missy nodded, a bit mystified that he'd known what she'd been thinking. "Everyone but you."

"I had a business emergency to deal with." His voice turned low. "And I was waiting for you."

A pang of...something she didn't wish to label hit her

right in the chest. She wrapped her arms across her middle against the chill that danced over her skin, raising goose bumps. The silky blazer and tank top she wore underneath were perfect for southern California in August, but the nights were cool here in Wyoming.

Yes, that had to be the reason for her body's reaction to Liam's words.

"Don't worry, it doesn't look anywhere near the same."

Again, meant for her ears only, and she knew exactly what he was talking about. "It's fine."

"A lot has changed since you were here—"

"Yes, of course, it has." She secretly hoped the attic space had been redone as extensively as Elise Murphy described. "As I said, it's fine. Wait—what is—" She stopped short and pointed at the dark object just outside the reach of the outdoor lighting. "Is that a helicopter on the other side of the lot?"

"It's for the family business," Liam said. "A couple of my brothers and I are the pilots."

She now remembered seeing something about it on the company's website, but she'd had no idea… "You fly, too?"

Liam grinned, gesturing with her suitcase, and Missy started walking again, her heels clicking against the stones. The sturdy pathway continued through the large grassy yard and forest of trees at the back of the house.

She wondered how far it went. Years ago there'd been only a dirt trail that led from the oversize backyard down to the river. When they rounded the corner of the house, Missy stumbled to a stop. "Oh, my."

"I told you things have changed a bit." Liam's voice flowed over her shoulder. "And I wasn't just talking about the boathouse."

She turned to him. "I can see that. I wasn't expecting—"

"Isn't it neat? You should see it in the daytime." Casey

spun around, coming dangerously close to the edge of an oversize in-ground pool. "They've got their own neighborhood back here!"

Yes, Missy could see that. The transformation of the yard was stunning.

"You might remember all we used to have was a simple wooden deck, but my folks wanted a complete outdoor entertainment space. Over the years they added the stone patio, fire pit, pool and the connecting pathways," he said as he led the way. "We boys built the gazebo back there to celebrate their fortieth wedding anniversary a few years ago. Mom said it was the perfect final touch."

Missy tried to take it all in. The care and thought that had gone into renovating the acreage was evident. Outdoor lights offered a soft glow, making it easy to see everything from the landscaping to the entertainment areas. Lighted pathways veered off in different directions through clusters of trees that gave each of the log homes a sense of privacy despite their relative closeness to each other.

"And the log homes," she said. "I'm guessing from what your mother said, you and your brothers all still live here."

"Not all of us. Adam has his own ranch down the road and Ric is currently stationed overseas, but yeah—" Liam grinned, and then shrugged. "I guess the rest of us figured the Murphy ranch was as good a place to settle down as anywhere else in town. At least we're not all still in the main house."

"Well, it's certainly big enough for everyone," she said, eyeing the house more closely.

Missy listened to him describe who lived where as they passed his brothers' homes, Casey a few steps ahead of them. The path sloped downward and led to the lake, and the trees got closer together. When the boathouse with its familiar wooden dock came into view, her stomach clenched.

"So that must leave this one as yours, right?"

Casey's question pulled Missy's gaze from the boathouse to a two-story log home that sat a bit farther back into the trees.

"Yes, that's my place," Liam said.

"Wow, it's big for one person. Since no one's mentioned it, I'm guessing you're not married."

"Casey!"

"It's okay." His gaze lingered on Missy for a moment before he looked at their daughter. "And you guessed correctly, I'm not. I was—twice, actually—but neither one stuck."

Twice? He'd married again? Not an unusual occurrence, but the news still surprised her.

"So do I have any younger half siblings running around?"

"Nope, just a handful of cousins, I'm afraid."

"Bugger, I always wanted a little sister." Casey shrugged and headed for the boathouse. "Used to bother my mum for years over that. Of course there was little chance of it happening. She rarely, if ever, dated after my father died."

Missy gasped and pressed a hand to her forehead, embarrassed at her daughter's directness but also to block out Liam's dark gaze as he turned to look at her. "Cassalyn Elizabeth—"

"Oh, it's never a good thing when she brings out the full name." Reaching the end of the boathouse, Casey jerked her thumb around the corner. "Your mum said stairs would lead up to the flat. Is this them?"

"Yes, a light should come on when you get to the top…" His voice trailed off as Casey disappeared, her footsteps echoing up the stairwell. "Is she avoiding me all of a sudden?"

"No, it's me she's trying to get away from." Missy couldn't stop from stealing glances at the beautiful front porch on Liam's home, so close now that it seemed to tower over them as they walked along the back side of the boathouse. "I apologize for her rudeness."

"Like I said, it's okay. I have a feeling she's going to have quite a few questions for us in the coming days."

"You're probably right." She followed him around the corner of the building, surprised when she saw a second-level porch had been added to the front of the boathouse that faced the water, creating a covered area over the three boat slips she remembered. "My, more changes."

"I told you."

"Yes, you did. Well, I should—" She stopped when the glow from the outdoor lighting suddenly disappeared, leaving them in darkness except for the light coming from the upper landing. "What—what just happened?"

"It must be ten o'clock. The lights are on a timed system with the majority of the accent features going off for the night. Don't worry—the outside lights on everyone's homes, as well as the pathways, are motion activated, in case you need anyone for…well, anything."

Meaning she was to go to him? The queen would give up the throne first. "Well, as I was saying, I should get upstairs and answer some of those questions."

Liam studied her in silence. Was he going to insist on being part of this discussion? Missy honestly didn't think she had the strength to include him, as terrible as that sounded.

Not after everything that had happened today.

Being back in Destiny, staying in the boathouse, standing so close to him she could reach out and touch—

"Yes, I guess you should," he finally said. "Let me take the bags up for you."

"I'll take them." Casey reappeared, clomping down the stairs. "Sorry for popping off like that. I think the time difference has me a bit knackered."

"If memory serves, that means tired, right?" Liam asked with a grin, handing over the luggage. "And apology accepted."

Casey smiled, and then turned to head back upstairs. "You coming, Mum? Wait until you see the loo! There's a giant claw-footed tub that sits in front of a huge glass window looking right out over the water."

Missy faltered, grabbing at the handrail as she started to follow. She swung her gaze back to Liam, even as she called after her daughter's departing figure. "There—there is?"

Liam retreated, the shadows not completely hiding the way his mouth lifted at one corner. "When I said it didn't look the same, I wasn't talking about the *entire* space. Some things are exactly how they used to be."

It was after midnight and she should be lost in dreamland, but Missy couldn't slow her mind enough to allow sleep to come.

Her talk with Casey had gone surprisingly well, her daughter handling the story of what happened all those years ago between Missy and Liam with ease. Of course, her anger with her grandparents was palpable, mixed with even more tears over her grandfather's recent death, leaving the poor girl confused about what she should be feeling.

Still, she seemed more interested in what had happened sixteen years ago here in Destiny. Missy shared some of what her time here had been like. But after one too many

yawns from Casey, Missy had pleaded exhaustion herself
and shooed her daughter off to the smaller of the apartment's two bedrooms.

After checking and finding her daughter sound asleep,
Missy then took that bubble bath she'd been longing for,
memories be damned. So what if the tub stood in the exact
same spot it had sixteen years ago?

The antique hadn't been in working order back then.
Not that they had let that stop them on a stormy afternoon,
lining the tub with old quilts and sharing a picnic there,
the roomy fixture big enough to fit both of them comfortably. So comfortably that they'd—

Okay, so the bubbles did little to relax her. Nor did the
cup of Earl Grey tea she'd made after finding a selection
of loose teas and a darling little pot in the cozy kitchen.

Setting the empty cup in the sink, Missy crossed the
parlor, drawn to the French doors that led to the covered
porch. She hoped a few moments in the fresh air would
clear away her whirlwind thoughts as she slipped outside,
closing the door behind her.

She tightened the sash on her dressing gown. The air
was cool as she walked to the porch railing, drawn by the
full moon lighting up the night sky and dancing over the
gentle current of the river-fed lake.

Leaning forward, she gazed up at the stars shining overhead, so clear and bright. Not a sight she saw often from
her London neighborhood. Years ago, her first glimpse at
a Wyoming sky at night had made her feel much as she
felt right now.

Lost and alone. Small. Insignificant. The same emotions that had swamped her the day she'd discovered she
was pregnant and had no idea who the baby's father was.

She'd prayed it was Liam. Hoped and prayed for weeks,
even after her parents and Stanford had learned about the

pregnancy. She'd debated constantly over getting in touch with Liam while having no idea how to explain the crazy situation.

Then she'd found out he'd married someone else. Trying not to allow her heart to be filled with pain and sorrow over the news had been hard. She hadn't wanted her baby to be stuck inside a body racked with such intense emotions for the remaining months of her pregnancy.

And she'd stopped hoping.

Now, fifteen years later, those long-ago prayers had been answered and their lives—hers, Casey's and Liam's—would never be the same.

Would it be fair to separate Casey and Liam so soon? Her daughter had pleaded to stay in Destiny, easily brushing aside the temptation of a month on a tropical beach in order to get to know the man who was her father. Her real father.

Casey and Stanford had never bonded, mostly because of his business schedule and a quiet disdain over Missy's refusal to hire a nanny. He had never gotten over the fact she had wanted to be the one to raise their child, even if it meant putting off her own schooling until Casey was older. Putting him and his career ambitions off, too, at times when it came to fancy parties or corporate travel. She had been a mother first, a wife second. Was it any wonder their marriage foundered after such a short time?

Casey had never seemed to miss having a father after Stanford's death, mainly because Missy's father had been such a doting presence in her life, especially when Missy and Casey had moved back home. To learn he'd played with their lives all those years ago damaged the memories both of them had of the man.

Missy sighed. Could she do it? Could she stay here at

Liam's home, where she'd be surrounded by the memories from a lifetime ago?

During her first visit to Destiny, she'd stayed with a family in town. The McIntyres had been nice people, even if their daughter had soon come to regret having to share her room. Not that it had mattered, because from the moment Missy and Liam had become a couple, her life had revolved around him, his family and the Murphy family home.

She'd traveled with the Murphys on weekends to the rodeos Liam and his brothers had competed in, marveling at his strength and commitment to the sport. A rising star on the rodeo circuit, Liam had been popular with everyone he came in contact with but still down-to-earth. So easy to talk to, to be with.

And she'd loved him. Loved all of them.

So much so that she'd turned her entire world upside down, provoking the wrath of her parents with her plan to go to college in America. It had taken time, but she'd managed to get everything in place so that she could surprise him—

"You bloody well surprised him, all right. Then he shocked you." Her whispered words filled the air, her fingers clutching the railing, nails biting into the wood as she rocked back and forth. "And nothing was the same after that."

A chill raced through her, whether from the night air or the fact that she was even more unsettled now than before she came out here, she didn't know. But it was time to head back inside.

When she turned around, a man leaning against a nearby post, barely visible in the dark, caught her eye. Missy gasped and stumbled backward, but then Liam was there, pulling her into his arms, steadying her.

"Are you okay?" he asked. "I didn't mean…"

His voice faded as she clutched at his wrinkled, unbuttoned dress shirt, the bare skin beneath hot to the touch. That same heat flowed through the silk of her gown from where his hands held her, igniting a burst of need deep inside her.

A swift intake of much needed air brought a clean, sharp, yet woodsy scent to her nose. A scent so familiar her stomach tightened at the memory.

"Missy?"

His features were still obscured by the shadows, but she could see a lock of dark hair falling forward as he stared down at her. It was as if the last sixteen years faded away and all she saw—felt—breathed—in front of her was the boy she'd once loved more than life itself.

A foolish love, childish infatuation, a crush.

A mistake.

That's what she'd been told after it ended, by her girlfriends, her parents. Labels she'd repeated often, come to believe, clung to, as the months and years passed. But while they'd been together…

Loving him, being loved by him, had been magical.

He pulled her closer, dipping his head. She responded by pressing up on her toes, her curves aligning to the solid wall of his chest, bringing her face even closer to his.

"Liam."

His name rushed past her lips in a hushed whisper. A low groan escaped from his seconds before his mouth landed on hers.

It was like coming home.

Chapter Four

This was not why he'd come here. He should have made his presence known when he'd first arrived. Surprised when the outside light hadn't come on, he'd paused, ready to call out to her, but had found himself leaning against the post at the top of the stairs as a way to get the crazy beating of his heart under control.

And yeah, so he could look at her, standing there, bathed in the moonlight, dressed in a silky bathrobe.

Then she'd spotted him.

Now, she was in his arms, rising to meet his mouth. She smelled the same, felt the same, and finally holding her caused that familiar electric charge to return, the same one that sang in his veins the moment she'd stepped from the car earlier tonight.

How was that possible after all this time? Why had he wanted her just like this, just this close, from the moment he'd seen her again? A woman who'd kept his daughter from him?

Not her fault. None of it.

Hard as it was to understand why parents would do that to their own child, he believed her story. And yet, she'd kept the possibility she might be carrying *his* child from him.

Shouldn't he be upset with her for that? Never mind that she planned to take Casey away again in just a few days.

None of that mattered at the moment, not when her lips trembled beneath his as he reacquainted himself with the taste of the first girl he'd ever loved.

Her fingers fisted in his shirt as she rose even higher to meet him, but it wasn't enough. He wanted more. Angling his head, he released her shoulders only so he could cup the softness of her cheeks with his palms.

He delved his fingers deep into her hair, itching to loosen the golden strands and see them tumble free. He traced the upper edge of her lips with his tongue, the fullness and shape of her mouth so familiar it was as if he'd just kissed her yesterday.

She gasped at his boldness, but before he could use that to his advantage, she wrenched from his embrace, shuffling backward, putting distance between them.

"What—what are you doing?" She lightly tapped her mouth. "Why did you do that?"

"I'm—" Liam paused, not having a ready answer to a valid question. "I wanted to keep you from falling."

"By kissing me?"

"That wasn't something I planned on happening." He started toward her, but stopped when she retreated again. "Why did you kiss me back?"

Her fingers paused against her lips, and then she dropped her hand. "It's late. Why are you here?"

Okay, no more talk about kissing. That was probably

for the best. "I saw you step outside. I wanted to make sure everything was okay."

"You saw me?"

He debated if he should keep what he'd discovered to himself, but honesty won out. "I never realized until tonight the view from my master bedroom allows me to look down and see much of the apartment."

Her eyes narrowed. "How much?"

"The main room, the kitchen and the porch."

"Did you see Casey and I—did you watch us when we were talking?"

He nodded again, deciding at that moment there'd already been enough deceit between them to last a lifetime. "How is she? She seemed a bit upset at times."

"She was, as I expected she would be, but in the end... I'd say she's handling all of it amazingly well." Missy's shoulders rose in a delicate shrug. "Then again, Casey has always been so easygoing about most things. I see now she must get that from—"

She bit hard on her bottom lip, cutting off her words.

"From me." Liam knew exactly what she'd been about to say. The comparison made his heart pound. "You were going to say she gets that from me."

"Well, she certainly doesn't get it from my side of the family." Missy walked toward the porch railing again, still keeping space between them, her gaze out on the water. "We Ellingtons are as uptight as you Yanks make all British people out to be."

He smiled, glad that she didn't seem to be in any hurry to go back inside. Mimicking her pose, he turned to look out over the lake, too, resting his forearms on the railing. "Oh, I don't know. I seem to remember you loosening up. Eventually."

"Eventually." She brushed back the hair the breeze

swept across off her face. "Being in Destiny was vastly different from what my life was like in London. It took me a long time to feel…comfortable."

"But not comfortable enough to stay." The moment the words popped out of his mouth, he wished he could take them back. The last thing he wanted tonight was to argue about the past. "Missy, I'm sorry. I shouldn't have said that."

"Well, an apology. How nice. Does that make up for the one I never got sixteen years ago?"

He looked at her, confused. "What?"

"Please don't tell me you've forgotten." She faced him. "About the plans I made? To go to college in Wyoming, jumping through hoops to make that happen. Giving up my placement in university back home, applying for a student visa, dipping into my trust fund to pay for it all. Not that any of that seemed to matter to you."

"It mattered. Of course, it mattered." He straightened and faced her. "And no, I never forgot. I also didn't have any idea what you were planning back then."

"I wanted to surprise you with the news that we would be able to be together. Instead, you surprised me—not to mention your entire family—when you announced you weren't going to college after all, but planned to be the next John Wayne."

"John Wayne never rodeoed, except in a movie or two, I think."

Missy rolled her eyes. "You know what I mean."

"Yes, okay, you surprised me that day, but in a good way." The memories of a hot July afternoon, not long after he'd taken the professional rodeo circuit by storm with an unexpected first-place showing at the Cody Stampede, came rushing back. "I wanted you to stay, was happy you were staying. I remember asking you to go on the road with me after I decided to rodeo full-time."

"As what?" Her voice rose, but then she glanced at the glass doors that led to the apartment and inched closer to him. "Your buckle bunny? Isn't that the quaint American saying? Not bloody likely."

Liam copied her low tone, even though he doubted Casey could hear them, as the bedrooms were on the other side of the apartment. "A fact you made very clear that day as you walked out."

"If memory serves, you made it clear you wouldn't miss me if I went back home."

"We were fighting. Hell, we were teenagers. Teenagers say stupid things."

"Yes, like you didn't care about me anymore. You were glad we were through."

"I lied," he shot back.

Taking a step forward, he remembered what she'd said earlier on the porch that triggered a forgotten memory. "Something I made clear in my letters to you."

Silence stretched between them as they stood there, almost as close as they'd been when he'd held her in his arms. Missy was breathing hard, her breasts rising and falling against the edges of her bathrobe.

Liam tried not to stare, but she was beautiful, as beautiful as ever, and a part of him liked that even after all this time, she was still so emotional about their relationship.

"Letters?" she finally asked. "What are you talking about?"

"I wrote to you, after you left." He shoved his hands in his pockets, causing his shirt to open even farther, but he had to do something to keep from reaching for her again. "Steve McIntyre, Suzanne's brother, got me your address from their folks."

Missy started to say something, but then pressed her lips together and remained silent.

"Hell, we were still in the dial-up stage of the internet back then and you didn't even have an email address. So I wrote to you, three times in fact, between July and October, after you left," he continued, remembering how he'd poured out his heart and soul in the same messy handwriting he still used today. "I never heard back from you."

"I never…" She averted her eyes, her gaze landing on his chest for a moment before she turned away. "I never got them. Any of them."

Of course she hadn't. A vile bitterness rose in his throat. He had to swallow it back before he spoke. "Your parents made sure of that."

She nodded, still not looking at him. "Yes, I suppose you're right."

More silence.

Liam dropped his head and closed his eyes. He hadn't planned on any of this—the kiss, talking about the past—when he'd headed over here. He'd been worried about Casey, about Missy, about how their talk had gone. He'd wanted to make sure she was okay, but he should have figured that the way things had ended between them all those years ago would come out sooner or later.

But with such feeling?

Her crack about his apology surprised him. Despite the years that had passed, everything that had happened the day they fought—everything between them during that year—still felt so real. To both of them, it seemed.

"I would've told you." Missy's fingers were cool where she touched his wrist, drawing his attention back to her. "If the test results—if the results I was shown had been different, had been the truth, I would have made sure you knew about your daughter. No matter what my parents might have wanted at the time."

He nodded, reading the truth in her eyes, but believing her butted up against the fact that she'd never had the chance. He'd never had the chance. "I would've done right by you, by Casey. As old-fashioned as that sounds."

"We were both teenagers and living half a world apart. I'm not sure how...what the right answer would have been for us back then." She sighed and dropped her hand. "Perhaps that was the logic behind my father's deceit."

She had a point, but that didn't mean they hadn't deserved to know the truth. "You two could have come back to Destiny."

"And what then? I would have followed you from rodeo to rodeo with a baby in my arms?"

"I wasn't only a cowboy back then. I earned my electrician's license after you left and worked for my father around my training and the rodeo competitions." Her attitude bugged him, even though they were talking about a past they couldn't change. "But your parents thought Stanford Dobbs was a better catch."

"I suppose they did." Missy took a step back, again folding her arms. "His family was in the same social circles as mine. He'd graduated from Oxford that same spring as Casey was born and was working at his father's investment firm by the time we married."

"A proper match for a proper English girl." A thought came to Liam. "Did he know the truth? Did your father ever tell your husband that Casey wasn't his daughter?"

"No." Her response was quick and firm, but then she caught her bottom lip with her teeth for a moment. "I don't think so...my goodness, it never occurred me to ask my mother that."

"Was he good to Casey?" *Good to you?* Liam wanted

to say that second part, but he managed to hold back the words.

"He was, even though he wasn't very involved with her daily care. Stanford worked long hours to provide for us. As he moved up in the company the busier he became and the more he traveled."

"So you were a full-time mother?"

She nodded. "Until Casey started school, which happened to be right about the time of Stanford's death. Casey and I moved back in with my parents and I was able to earn my degree in three years."

Liam added the years in his head. "I was getting my master's degree at the same time."

"Hmm, yes, I know. Casey showed me the write-up in the rodeo program about you. She read to me about both your rodeo career and your time with the family business. I'll admit I was surprised to learn you only competed professionally for three years."

Liam reached inside his open shirt and rubbed at his left shoulder. The phantom burning sensation was in his head—he knew that—but sometimes he'd swear he could still feel the lightning-hot pain.

Even after all this time. Especially now.

"Not even. I was halfway through my third season, holding tight to the number-one ranking, when I shattered my left arm, from the shoulder down past the elbow, after getting thrown by a horse named Destiny Changer, of all things. Sure changed things for me."

"And you never rode again?"

"Not as a saddle bronc rider." He pushed his cotton shirt off his shoulder, baring the rigid scarring to the moonlight. To her. "Took me almost a year just to get full use of my arm again."

A soft gasp escaped past Missy's lips as her gaze flittered over his skin, taking in the evidence of his injury. "Oh, my. It's…it's not what I expected."

"That's one way to put it."

"No." Her eyes flew up to meet his. "I'm sorry, I was talking about your tattoo."

"Oh, that." Liam glanced down at the black silhouette design that covered most of his left pectoral—an image of a saddle bronc rider, right in the middle of the craziness during the eight seconds of a cowboy trying to stay astride the horse. He righted his shirt and closed a couple of the buttons. "Yeah, I got that a few years afterward. I was tired of seeing nothing but scars every time I looked in the mirror."

"But the location—" She paused. "I mean, it's right over your heart."

"Yeah, well, being a cowboy was all I had, all I loved at the time. Even if it was lost to me forever."

It hurt to say the words, but it had been the truth at the time.

That first year in college following his official retirement from the rodeo circuit found him more often drunk than sober, barely getting to his classes and alienating everyone from his family to old rodeo buddies who'd tried to stay in touch.

He'd been lost in a world of self-indulgent pity over the way his life had turned out at the ripe old age of twenty-one, while Missy had been busy raising their daughter as another man's wife.

Damn, they still had so much to talk about, but it was late.

"I should head back," he said, "and let you get some rest."

"Yes, that would be…good. It's been a long day."

He read exhaustion in her eyes, in the drop of her shoulders. The need to pull her into his arms again, to comfort her this time, was so strong he took a step back.

"Well, good night then," he said instead, heading for the stairs. Pausing at the top step, he gestured over his shoulder. "I don't know what happened to the light out here, but I'll check on it tomorrow."

"My fault, I fear. I must have mishandled the switches in the kitchen while learning my way. Will fix that straight away when I go back inside."

"Okay, then. I'll see you both tomorrow." The small talk was inane, but his feet refused to move. "Or rather, later today."

She nodded. "Right. Later today."

Don't look at her and you might be able to get your ass out of here! He listened to the internal command, focused on the stairs and started down. "Good night, again."

"I've decided we're staying."

He froze, his gaze darting back to her. "You are?"

"We have a month or so before we need to be back in London, when Casey's second school term begins." Hands clasped against her stomach, Missy came a few steps closer. "That should be long enough to get back test results… Of course, we can make other arrangements to stay in town—"

"You'll stay here." He cut her off, elation racing through his veins that she and Casey were going to be in Destiny, were going to be at his family's home, at least for now. "The apartment is yours for as long as you want it. Mom will insist on it."

"But most of our luggage is still at the hotel in LA. I'm not quite sure how we go about getting it here."

"I'll get Katie on it," Liam said, adding the item to the mental list of things he needed to take care of in the morning. "First thing tomorrow."

"Katie?"

"She's the office manager for the company. Believe me, the woman can work wonders. You won't have any issues canceling your vacation rental?"

Missy joined him at the landing. With him two steps down, their gazes were even. "The use of the beachside villa was a thank you from a producer friend at the film studio where I work. I'll let him know of our change of plans tomorrow."

Liam brushed aside the flicker of annoyance her words created. So her friend was a man. Big deal. She probably had a lot of male friends.

Casey had made that crack about her mother not dating much, answering his unspoken question about whether she'd ever married again.

Hell, he'd given it a second go himself right after college and failed miserably for the second time. Not that he'd led the life of a monk since then, but after just having this woman in his arms, his mouth on hers, the last thing he wanted to think about was a friendship that netted her the use of a Hawaiian beach house.

No, what he wanted was to lean over the railing, wrap his hand around the back of her head and bring her mouth down to his.

Bad idea. Not when he had just gotten what he really wanted. A chance to get to know Casey. To get to know Missy, again...

Yeah, not helping, man.

He blinked away that thought to find her still standing there, watching him. She had something else she wanted to say. He was sure of it, but her staring at him while swiping at her bottom lip with the tip of her tongue wasn't helping his resolve to get out of here.

"Was there anything else?" he asked.

She nodded, but remained silent.

"What?" he pushed, something telling him he wasn't going to like it. "Missy, after everything we've—said to each other tonight, you can just spit it out."

She pulled in a deep breath, releasing it in a slow exhale before she said, "Destiny seems to be the same quaint small town I remember. I'm sure the gossipmongers are already talking about my daughter's appearance at the rodeo tonight with you and your family."

"You're probably right."

"I wonder whether you've decided what you plan to tell…people. Your family, friends, colleagues. Now that you know everything."

Another good question that he didn't have a ready answer to. "What do you want me to tell them?"

"The truth. All of us have been living with this lie for too long."

Liam admired how she spoke without any hesitation, but the last thing he wanted was to cause her any embarrassment over what her parents had done. To her. To them. Especially since she'd had so little time yet to come to terms with their deception herself.

"We'll tell them…" He paused, and then went with a decision straight from his gut. "We'll tell anyone who asks there was a mix-up with the hospital paperwork and your… husband was incorrectly listed as Casey's father. The mistake wasn't discovered until now."

Relief colored her features, but she still appeared upset. "It won't take a math genius to figure out the time difference between when I left here, Casey's birth and what I did when I got home to create such a…possibility."

"I don't care about that."

When Liam let himself think about it, the idea of Missy getting busy with her ex still stung a bit, but hell, that was years ago. With everything going on between them now—especially in the last half hour—her actions back then just added another twist in this crazy turn his life had taken.

"So, you believe me then?" she asked. "This whole crazy story?"

Liam looked at her. His first love. Now the mother of his child. "That's why we're getting a new DNA test done, right? Don't worry, everything will be okay."

He took a step, intent on heading down the stairs, but apparently Missy wasn't done.

"I told you earlier how Casey was taking all of this in stride," she said, "but as excited as she is about you and what you represent, she has no idea how you feel about suddenly having a teenage daughter in your life."

The pounding in his chest returned.

All the things he hadn't been able to experience over the past fifteen years when it came to Casey flashed inside his head. Birthdays. Holidays. Her first words, first steps, first day of school.

"Seeing how I've only known about her for the last twelve hours or so, I'm not sure exactly what I'm feeling, either, but we'll work on that."

"She wants to get to know you, and your family."

"I want that, too."

The words came easily because they were true. He wanted to get to know his daughter. Wanted her to be a part of his life, part of his family. What that meant for him and Missy, he had no idea.

He'd honestly never thought—

Okay, maybe once in a while, especially lately with the company's business growing in the UK the way it was, he'd thought that he might someday run into his first love again on a trip to London. Pass her in Piccadilly Circus. Catch sight of her in a restaurant or on the subway.

Now she was here, right in front of him.

Now he had the chance to get to know her all over again...

"As for all that happened here tonight, between us—" Missy turned slightly and waved at the porch behind her, before putting her hand on the doorknob "—I know talking about the past—our past—is inevitable. Reliving it, however, is not. I'm only staying in town for Casey's sake. To give her what she wants and needs."

And that was all.

She disappeared back inside the apartment. It was as if she'd read his mind and taken care of answering his unasked question. It was for the best, he decided as he headed back to his house.

All fantasies aside, the last thing he needed right now was to get involved with anyone, least of all Missy. He lived and breathed his position as CEO of Murphy Mountain Log Homes, and now he'd had fatherhood tossed into his lap.

Besides, his track record proved he wasn't a settling-down kind of guy.

But was he father material?

He loved his niece and nephews, enjoyed spending time with them, even the baby. Not that Casey needed him that way, but with the other kids he liked helping with their homework. Taking them and their friends for rides in the company helicopter. Going to their games. He'd even ended up teaching Abby how to drive this past spring after she and her father disagreed over who was at fault for a toppled tombstone in the town's cemetery during one of their lessons.

How hard could it be to have the same relationship with Casey? He had no idea. But one thing he did know was that he only had a month to make that happen.

Chapter Five

They were staying! At least for the rest of their holiday.

Unfortunately, in less than six weeks, she'd be back in London, suiting up in a plaid skirt, navy blue blazer and ugly oxfords.

And she'd have to get rid of the blue and pink streaks. Her piercings would have to go too. Gah. She would be ordinary…again. Worst of all, they'd be back living with her grandmum.

Or maybe not. After everything that had gone on in the last few weeks, Casey didn't have a clue what was going to happen when they returned to London.

For now she was glad to be in Destiny with Liam Murphy.

Her real dad.

The man who sat directly across from her with a big smile on his face, stuffing his fourth hot dog into his mouth. Four! Crikey, he was big, but still. He had to be at least six feet tall and sitting there next to her mum, he made her look small and delicate.

She studied Liam while he and her mum chatted. Casey and he looked a lot alike—their baby pictures could have been carbon copies—but she now noticed she and Liam shared height and the same eye color too.

Eyes that were constantly in her mum's direction. Like right now.

"You see, ending a tour of Destiny with a late lunch was the right thing to do." Liam's words cut into her thoughts as he wiped at his mouth with a napkin. "You never could resist a whistle pig."

"It's still a silly name for a food item." Her mum blushed as she lightly scrubbed the crumbs from her fingers over her now empty plate. "Even for the best hot dog I've eaten in years."

"I don't think I've ever seen you eat a hot dog before." Casey finished the last of her own beef frank, deliciously wrapped in bacon and smothered in cheese, then mumbled around the last bite, "Much less two of them."

They sat at a picnic table outside a fast food restaurant named after their lunch, a place that had an oversize dancing cartoon pig with a whistle around its neck on the marquee.

"She's got you fooled. I remember her downing four of these."

Liam grinned as he spoke, sending a wink in her direction that made Casey feel sort of gooey inside.

"I ate those on a dare and I was honking the whole next day." Missy reached for her drink, pausing just before putting the straw between her lips to stare at Casey. "Don't even think about it, young lady, and it's not polite to talk with your mouth full."

Casey swallowed, and then laughed. Blimey, that felt good.

"So, what now?" Liam asked. "Anything you're interested in doing or seeing? Or should we head back to the family compound?"

"Do you have to go back to work?" Not that he'd really been away from it as his cell phone chimed for the umpteenth time since they'd left the house. "Again? That thing is worse than Mum's!"

He grabbed his phone and looked at the screen. "Sorry, but I need to take this. I'll be just a minute."

After a few minutes, Liam returned. When her mum said they should head to the house, he shot Casey a questioning look. She answered with a casual shrug and headed for his truck.

It was bloody hot when they got back to the Murphy compound. Maybe she'd sit on the dock and dangle her toes in the lake. Or perhaps the twins were around and they could hang out, but when they rounded the corner into the yard, they found a crowd gathered on the deck and around the pool.

"Hey, you're back," Adam called from where he sat beneath a shaded umbrella table. His wife and parents were happily passing the baby back and forth between them. Bryant and his wife, Laurie, sat nearby in matching lounge chairs.

"We need a few more bodies if we're going to get up a game."

"Yeah, Uncle Liam! Grab your swim trunks!"

"Yeah, come join us!"

"Your uncle is probably going to disappear into his office, boys." Nolan talked over his boys' excited cries, the three of them already in the shallow end of the pool, setting up a floating volleyball net. Nolan stopped long enough to peer over the top of his sunglasses. "He's a busy man with lots of work. Isn't that right, Uncle Liam?"

Casey looked over at her fath—at Liam. She was ready

to race to the boathouse and slip on her bathing suit, but it sounded as if Liam didn't usually join in the fun with the rest of his family. Did that mean she and her mum shouldn't?

Liam smiled, and then turned to Casey and Missy. "How about it? You two have swimsuits?"

"Packed in our luggage in LA, I'm afraid," her mum said, her gaze unreadable behind her dark sunglasses. "Sorry."

"I've got one with me," Casey piped up, obviously catching her mum by surprise.

"Why don't you and I go and get changed, Casey? Your mother can relax and enjoy the sunshine." Liam gestured toward the deck. "If we can get her to peel off a few layers."

"My layers are just fine." Missy squared her shoulders. "Thank you."

Casey headed for the boathouse, hurrying ahead of Liam, his mobile once again at his ear. It didn't matter now. She didn't want to talk to him, not when it was just the two of them.

Not yet, anyway.

After she'd changed into her suit and lathered on sunscreen, she followed the path back to the pool. She could hear the laughter and everyone talking but slowed when she noticed Abby lying on a lounge chair at the opposite end of the patio area. She wasn't alone. Casey recognized the other girls as the ones Abby had gone off with at the rodeo. They must have just arrived.

"Can you believe they're staying? In the boathouse?" Abby's voice carried over the yard easily enough to hear, but Casey doubted anyone else could at the other end of the pool. "Up until yesterday none of us even knew about her. My uncle has got to be flipping out—"

"Uh, hi there." One of the girls, a pretty brunette, cut Abby off by calling out to Casey while removing her sunglasses to squint at her. "You must be Abby's new cousin."

Should Casey give the girls a simple nod and keep walking? But that would mean giving her cousin and her snarky comments the satisfaction of running her off. Not bloody happening.

She crossed the grass, hoping she looked more casual than the firecrackers banging around inside her stomach. "Yes, I'm Casey Dobbs."

"Abs says you're from England."

"That's right. London, actually."

"Cool accent. I'm Valerie and this is Jannie." The brunette introduced herself and her friend while Abby pointedly ignored her, continuing with her lotion application. "Do you mind if I ask you a question?"

Casey wondered where this might be going. "No, go ahead."

"Did that hurt?" Valerie tapped the side of her nose. "Getting it, I mean."

Ah, the diamond stud. She shrugged. "No, it wasn't too bad."

"What about the rest of the holes in your head?" Abby asked. "You must have at least a dozen piercings in your ears."

Ah, the snarkiness continued. "Thirteen, actually. Seven on the right, six on the left."

"Hey, that's cool."

Casey looked over and saw Logan and Luke had swum down to the end of the pool and propped their arms on the edge, but for the life of her she didn't know which one was which.

"Don't mind Abby," the twin who spoke continued.

"She's pissed our dad won't let her get a third set. Or the belly button ring she wants."

"Zip it, Luke," Abby snapped at her brother and then turned back to Casey. "So, thirteen..." She dropped her chin, pulled the dark shades down to the bridge of her nose and stared. "That's supposed to mean something?"

"It's my lucky number."

"Why am I not surprised," Abby deadpanned, and then hesitated before righting her glasses and collapsing against the lounge chair, stretching out her legs, pointed toes and all.

Her friends giggled. Their dismissal stung. Casey took a step backward, determined to walk away with head held high, but then the twins scurried out of the pool and quickly jumped back in, side by side, causing a spray of water to hit the patio and the edge of the lounge chairs.

"Knock it off, you two!" Abby called out, kicking one perfectly manicured foot at her brothers. "We don't want to get wet."

Casey eyed the trio of American beauties with their perfectly tanned limbs and perfectly coiffed hair. She dropped her stuff onto the last remaining chair, toeing off her shoes. Pulling her shirt over her head first, she reached for the zipper on her shorts.

"Hey, Casey!" the boys called from the water. "You coming in?"

"Of course." A quick shimmy and her shorts fell to the ground. She stepped out of them and before she allowed herself to think twice, raced toward the pool. "Budge up!"

Launching into the air, she tucked her body into a tight ball, wrapping her arms around her knees seconds before she plunged into the water—kersploosh!—making what she hoped was a spectacular splash with far-reaching effects.

Her feet touched the bottom and she opened her eyes, did a swift five count and pushed off, breaking the surface to find the twins cheering for her.

Abby and her crew? Not so much, as their outraged shrieks filled the air.

"Casey."

She spun, surprised to find Liam standing at the edge of the pool.

"Pretty impressive. But was that really necessary?" he asked as he went to rejoin the adults.

She blamed the sudden stinging in her eyes on the chlorine. Pushing her hair back from her face, she schooled her features into a practiced air of innocence. "Oh, bugger, did I do that?" Casey called out. "Sorry, mate."

Abby's glare was lethal, and her friends didn't look too happy either as they toweled off, but then a male voice called Abby's name and the girl's transformation from a wet hen to a purring kitten was striking.

As was the bloke heading toward her.

He was tall and had a killer smile, his cropped straw-colored hair and wide shoulders making him stand out from the two boys with him.

"I found this on the bleachers," the cutie said, holding out a sweatshirt to Abby. "You must've forgotten it after cheerleading practice."

"Really?" Abby reached for the item with what looked like a genuine smile. "I have no idea how that could've happened."

Sincere smile or not, Casey rolled her eyes at her cousin's sickening sweet tone. She climbed out of the pool, the water dripping from her body. "Practice? Don't tell me rodeos have cheerleaders."

Six pairs of eyes swung in her direction. Interest flared

from the boys while the girls' combined glances bordered on wicked.

"We cheer for our school's football team," Valerie said.

"Ah, right." She strolled forward and held out a hand toward the tall lad. "Hello, I'm Casey. Abby's cousin from England."

"Hi." Confusion crossed his face as he glanced between her and Abby, but then he took her hand. "I'm Nathan Lawson." After a quick elbow from one of his friends he added, "This is J.T. and Cody. Abby never said anything about having family from the UK."

"Believe me, she's a surprise. Sort of an oops, you might say."

"So, football." Casey ignored Abby's dig and smiled at the boys after releasing Nathan's hand.

"Well, not the kind of football you're used to," Nathan said. "We're talking American football, not soccer."

"I understand." Casey smiled as a shiver raced through her. "But I did enjoy a game of American football at Wembley. Those Patriots certainly played a good match."

"You went to the NFL game between the New England Patriots and the St. Louis Rams in London?" Nathan asked.

"Oh, yes. My mum and I had box seats thanks to—well, someone she worked with."

"Sweet. What does your mom do that she gets perks like that?" J.T. asked.

"She's a costume designer for a movie studio."

"Really?" Jannie stepped closer, not seeing how Abby's eyes narrowed in her direction. "Have you met anyone famous?"

Wrapping a towel around her waist like a sarong, Casey pushed the water from her hair, squeezing out the ends. "I met Johnny Depp once."

Both Valerie and Jannie gasped.

"You've met Johnny Depp?" they asked, voices in harmony.

"Last summer. On a film location in Paris. He was the one who gave us the tickets to the football game."

"Oh, my God, really?" Valerie asked.

Casey nodded. "He and Emma Watson were—"

"Wait, you met Emma Watson, too?" Cody interrupted her. "That hot chick from the Harry Potter movies?"

"Yes, she was there, too." Her gaze collided with Abby's dark stare and she knew what was coming. "Would you like to see pictures?"

Surprise flared in Abby's eyes. Feeling victorious, Casey got her phone. The kids gathered around as she showed off the images and answered their rapid-fire questions.

Abby joined the circle, but remained silent.

Chapter Six

"She's ignoring me."

Liam's quiet words pulled Missy's attention away from the beautiful open fields and distant thickly forested foothills of the Laramie Mountains that made up his brother's ranch.

It had been sixteen years since she'd last been on a horse, but it felt good, familiar, even, in a way that surprised her more than she expected. Maybe because the cowboy next to her had been the one who'd taught her how to ride.

Earlier today, when Liam had swung into the saddle with a grace and ease that reflected his years as a cowboy, Missy had been as awestruck as when she was a teen. A dark Stetson, similar to the one he'd always worn during competitions, shaded his face. He held the reins loosely in one hand while his powerful legs instinctively commanded the animal beneath him without his having to say a single word.

She'd stared at him like a daft cow!

Thank goodness she'd already mounted her ride. In fact, the places where he'd touched her as he helped with the stirrups still tingled. She rubbed her fingertips across the spot on her jeans-clad thigh again, pausing when Liam glanced her way.

"I don't believe Casey is ignoring you," Missy finally said, purposely laying her hand flat against her leg. She focused instead on her daughter, who rode ahead of them. "She's paying attention to Adam's instructions and trying desperately not to look like she's hanging on for dear life."

Liam turned away, his gaze on Casey now, an easy smile on his face. "She's a natural. Scampered right up into the saddle before I could even help her."

"Eager and determined to learn with a healthy dose of bravado. That's Casey. Besides, you were busy reintroducing me to riding on the other side of the corral while Adam was instructing her."

"You're a natural, too." He looked at Missy again, his eyes warm and the smile still there, but now his lips held a hint of something…more…causing a fluttering deep inside her. "You haven't forgotten anything I taught you all those years ago."

"Well, you taught me a lot back then."

Did he ever.

Being with Liam had introduced her to a whole new world of fun, freedom and the flush of a first love. She'd been surprised to find out he was as inexperienced as she, although having barely kissed a boy until she met him, she had been the real innocent. At least until he'd showed her so many wonderful things with the way he kissed her, touched her, made love to her…

Missy blinked hard, having no idea how her thoughts had gone from horseback riding to…well, to *that*. Then again, in less than forty-eight hours in the man's company, it had only taken one moment in his arms and she'd known exactly why she was having these thoughts, these feelings—

Memories. That's all they were. All they would be.

Giving her head a quick shake as if to empty her mind, she caught Liam's grin, almost as if he knew what she'd been thinking.

Tugging on the brim of the straw hat she'd borrowed from Adam's wife, who'd stayed behind with their napping baby, she planned to blame the heated blush racing across her cheeks on the afternoon sun.

"I meant you taught me a lot about riding back then, when your family still had horses at your place."

Liam looked at her for a long moment. He then leaned forward and gently patted the neck of the beautiful buckskin quarter horse he rode. "Yes, we did have a full stable years ago. Once Adam got his place up and running, he took the few we had left to his ranch. Danny Boy being one of them."

"It was nice of Adam and Fay to invite us for a visit. Their place is lovely."

"Casey told Adam yesterday she wanted to learn how to ride," Liam said, his smile gone again. "After getting Bryant to agree to take her for a spin in the helo."

So they were back to this. Goodness, he sounded almost jealous of his brothers and how they were taking to Casey.

"And when Abby's friends took over the pool after beating us old guys at volleyball and then stuck around for dinner afterward…"

"A teenager choosing to spend time with people her own age instead of her parents," Missy teased when his voice faded. "Shocking."

"Does she think of me as a parent?"

Do you think of her as a daughter?

"Wow, would you listen to me," he said, pulling ahead and guiding his horse across a section of a slow-moving creek with hers splashing right behind. Adam and Casey far ahead now, barely visible in the cottonwood trees that dotted the landscape. "You two have only been here a few days. She doesn't even know me as a person, much less anything more."

She could see Liam's concern was genuine, and it touched her heart. More than it probably should. Then again, everything about Liam affected her more than it should.

Missy thought back to yesterday afternoon, when everyone had gathered at the pool. To how she'd been gobsmacked the moment Liam had returned to the backyard wearing the same polo shirt as earlier but sporting a pair of dark swim trunks that hung low on his hips.

He'd spotted her gawking, of course.

With a grin, he'd walked over to her and they'd talked for a few minutes—about what, she had no idea, as her brain had emptied the moment he stood up, pulled off his shirt and dropped it to the cushion next to her.

A calculated move on his part, she was sure, just as the stop at the eatery they'd frequented as teens had been, but still, she'd been unable to look away as he dived into the pool, disappearing beneath the water before rising again like a Greek god, muscles glistening in the sun, his tattoo standing out in stark relief against his tanned skin—

"Missy?"

She looked up and found Liam pointing at her and then at her ride. "Sorry, woolgathering. Did you say something?"

"You might want to ease up on the bit unless you want

her to stop altogether. You're clutching those reins as if your life depends on it."

Blimey, girl, get a hold of yourself!

Embarrassed at her inability to keep her thoughts centered on their conversation about their daughter, she cursed her fair English skin for the second time today as heat flooded her cheeks.

Easing her grip, Missy dipped her head and offered her riding companion a quick neck rub as an apology. "Sorry about that, girl. I am a wee bit out of practice, and that creek was deeper than I expected."

"You okay now?"

"Right as rain." She took a moment, keeping her attention on the horse as she pulled in a steadying breath before looking up again. "I was thinking about yesterday and wondering if Casey said or did something that makes you certain she's shutting you out."

"I don't know." Liam shrugged, their horses now side-by-side again. "The cheek swab...went okay? You were there. Did she seem bothered by it?"

Missy shook her head.

"And she talked while we drove around afterward, asking us a lot of questions. But once Abby and her friends joined us in the pool, she seemed to shut me out," he continued. "Ah, hell. Maybe that's typical teenage stuff— being embarrassed by the adults—and I'm being stupid."

"No, you're not."

From the moment Missy had found out about the doctored DNA test, a part of her had been worried that Liam might reject Casey, want nothing to do with her. To hear that after such a short time he was worried about her rejecting him, she found herself wanting desperately to make him feel better.

"I know we haven't shared much about our lives in London, but back home, her world is much more…contained. She has just a few close girlfriends, suffered through her first broken heart over a boy last year and other than my parents, I'm her only family. Now, with my father's death and what we've learned since then…it's been a great deal for her to take in. She just needs time to adjust."

"Yeah, I can understand that."

"And like most teenagers, she can go from being cheeky to tears and back again in a matter of minutes. I think she's excited to be here, to meet you and your family, but then maybe she remembers the reason why…"

Missy let her voice trail off when she realized she was talking about herself as well.

"We're going to be around for the next month or so. Give her some time," she continued, her tone gentle. "As I said, being in America, in Destiny, with you…is all new to her. There is so much to see and do and take in. It must be overwhelming. Much like when I took her to Disneyland Paris for the first time, I suspect."

"So I'm being compared to an amusement park?" Liam laughed. "What's that make me? The Dumbo ride?"

Missy was glad to see his smile return. She pretended to ponder his question for a moment, and then grinned back. "I would say you're more like Space Mountain."

"Yeah? Why's that?"

"One part imposing, one part scary and one part thrilling. But in the end I'm sure she'll come to believe the ride was worth it."

Liam reached out and caught Missy's horse's reins in his hand, pulling them to a stop in the dense shade of a grove of trees. "Do I scare you?"

Yes.

She curbed the impulse to go with that answer and instead replaced it with another. "No, not anymore. Perhaps you did at one time, but that—"

"Was a long time ago."

Liam finished her sentence with her, their words tangling together.

Seconds later, he'd maneuvered his horse closer until his leg brushed against hers. "Well, lady, you scare the hell out of me."

She pretended not to notice how her body tingled with awareness at his nearness, how the clean male scent of him invaded her head or how he spoke in the present tense. "Way back when?"

Pushing up the front brim of his Stetson with a finger, he leaned in close and slowly shook his head. "Nope, right now. Right here."

"You know, for a guy who just found out he's a dad, you're handling all of this very well."

Liam looked up from the piles of paperwork littering his desk and found Nolan lounging comfortably on the leather sofa on the other side of his office. A spot where Liam often woke up when his days ended long past sunset and he was too tired to walk back to his place.

Speaking of time...

He glanced at his watch. It was after five o'clock already. End of the workday for most, but not him. He'd planned to go find Casey and her mother at lunchtime today, but then he'd been reminded about the rodeo committee follow-up meeting in town and that had kept him out of the office for the rest of the afternoon.

Now he was playing catch-up by multitasking—sitting in on a conference call, checking email and printing job proposals—while wondering what Missy and Casey had done to occupy themselves on this gray and gloomy afternoon.

He hadn't been able to get them out of his head all day.

"Yeah, how do you manage—"

This time it was Bryant who spoke, breaking into his thoughts, but Liam cut him off with a swift karate chop in the air. When he got a raised eyebrow in return, he tapped the earpiece he wore, signaling he was still on the phone.

Bryant, who had walked in not long after Nolan and now sat with a glass of whiskey in his hand, only shrugged, but Nolan straightened, dropping his feet to the floor.

"That conference call with the Becketts is still going on?" he asked. "What's it about?"

Thankful for the mute button, Liam shrugged and turned to the large monitor on the right side of his desk. "I honestly couldn't tell you. I zoned out after the missus started in on the wall color of bathroom number five."

"Then why are you—"

"Because her husband is a major player in Silicon Valley and we just built them a multimillion-dollar getaway in Jackson Hole, that's why."

Liam put aside his thoughts of Missy and Casey for the moment so he could finish up the two emails he had open and send the latest round of contract proposals to the printer in the outer office.

It was then he realized the silence in his ear meant the tech wizard's wife was waiting for an answer to a question he hadn't heard.

He reached up and pressed a button. "Sorry, but I missed that last part…" Pausing, he listened this time, the question making him scrub hard at the back of his neck. "Well, perhaps you're going about choosing the colors all wrong."

His brothers cringed at the same moment he did. Okay, that came out wide of the mark.

"What I meant was, instead of using a piece of art or fabric as your inspiration, look for something more personal." He then remembered what he'd overheard Missy say to his mother at brunch yesterday while talking about her work. "Start with your wardrobe. You always look fabulous, Felicia. You wear your favorite colors. Why not use the same ones in your home?"

Bryant and Nolan's expressions went from uncomfortable to confused, but the feminine voice in his ear was happy. "I'm glad I could help," he said. "Yes, we'd love to see the place when you and Philip have your open house. Please feel free to add us to your guest list."

He ended the call, yanked the miniature headset from his ear and set his office line to go directly to Katie or to voice mail, knowing the major players had his cell phone number and wouldn't hesitate to call if needed.

Leaning back into his chair, he sighed and closed his eyes.

"Start with your wardrobe?" Nolan snorted. "Where did you come up with a crazy idea like that?"

Before Liam could answer, he heard the distinct sound of high heels on hardwood. He opened his eyes, and for a moment thought it might be—

Katie walked into the office, looking as pulled together as she had at the start of the day, in a dress covered with red flowers that matched the red of her hair. She was carrying his printouts.

"Don't listen to him, boss man," she said. "It was a great idea."

"How did you hear me out in the hall?" Nolan asked.

"Your voice carries. A whisperer you're not." She waited while Liam cleared a space by shoving aside a pile of folders.

"I know that was a last-minute call," he said, taking the

paperwork from her, "but please tell me you had time to record it or listened in to take notes."

"I listened. The transcript is already in their online folder."

Katie stood there, hands clasped, and Liam grinned, knowing the mess on his desk was driving their anal-retentive office manager crazy. Neat and orderly should be the woman's middle name—she kept the inner workings of Murphy Mountain Log Homes just that.

"You sticking around for dinner?" he asked, knowing his mother probably already made the invite.

Katie shrugged and headed for the door. "Sure. I've got nothing else planned." She stopped and then turned around, her expression pained. "I'm sorry. That was terrible of me."

Liam looked at his brothers. Bryant seemed as surprised by her words as he was, but Nolan's gaze was glued to the Persian rug beneath his feet as if he was memorizing the pattern.

Liam swung his gaze back to her. "You're always welcome, you know that, but you don't have to stay for dinner."

Katie's smile lacked its usual brilliance. "I know, but seeing how I've got nothing in my kitchen but leftovers from Sherry's Diner and a half dozen moving boxes, I'll stay."

She left the room, the clinking of her fancy shoes echoing behind her.

"Moving boxes?" Liam turned to his brothers again, but Bryant only shrugged. "Nolan? What's going on?"

"Katie moved out of Jake's place this weekend," his brother said, his gaze now on the empty fireplace. "She's back in an apartment in town."

Liam knew she'd been seeing one of the local sheriff's deputies for over a year and had been excited about moving in with him and his two young girls. "Didn't she give up her place a month or so ago to be with him and the kids?"

Nolan nodded. "Yeah, but I guess Jake and his wife decided to reconcile just before signing the divorce papers. The house is on the market and the man was smart enough to move himself and the girls to wherever his wife went after she first took off."

"What a lousy thing to do." Bryant finished his drink and headed for the bar. "No wonder Katie was in such a bad mood last week, not to mention absent from the barbecue on Saturday."

The anger burning in Liam's gut slowly morphed into guilt. He'd been so busy with the rodeo preparations last week and then with Missy and Casey showing up, he hadn't noticed anything was wrong. Or Katie's absence this weekend—she, Jake and the girls had often joined the family in the past.

"Is she going to be okay?" he asked.

"Oh, you know Katie," Nolan offered dryly. "She always finds someone new."

True, she had dated a number of men over the years, but this time it had seemed pretty serious. Serious enough that she'd moved in with the man. "Maybe she needs some time off."

"I offered. She turned me down." Nolan sat back, leg bent, propping a foot on his knee. "Asked if she needed any help moving, too, once I managed to get her to tell me what was wrong. She said she was all set."

Liam nodded, making a note to keep an eye on her as he stared at the latest contracts, mentally calculating how many he could get through after dinner. "So, is Adam here yet? I'm guessing he went home to get Fay and the baby after work."

"Haven't seen him, but what's with this family dinner?" Nolan asked. "We were all just together two days ago."

"Maybe Mom pulled it together for Katie." If anyone knew about the goings-on in Destiny, it was their mother. She had the town wired, her roots deep in the local gossip, especially now that she'd mastered the art of tweeting.

"Or maybe not." Bryant fumbled the crystal stopper but managed to get it back into the bottle. "You know Mom. Always looking for a reason to have the entire family together."

Liam shared a look with Nolan, who shook his head in reply, showing he was clueless.

Something else was up. Bryant was never nervous.

The man was a freak for numbers, with a laid-back personality that bordered on sedentary. Which was a good thing in his position as the company's chief financial officer. Their folks had always said he was their lull in the storm after the havoc caused by their first four boys. Then, of course, Ric had come along and the family had been complete.

"What's bugging you?" Liam asked.

"Nothing." Bryant stared into the glass for a moment, and then set it down untouched. "How do you do it?"

Confused, Liam glanced at Nolan, who again shook his head. "Do what?"

Bryant turned to face him. "Like Nolan said earlier. How do you stay so effing calm when a daughter you've never met—never even knew about—suddenly shows up at your front door?"

Surprised by his brother's tone, Liam sat back in his chair. Was he pissed? No, Bryant sounded almost anxious.

"Since nothing like this has ever happened to me before," he finally said. "I'm not sure how I'm supposed to act."

"I guess being a father is going to come as easy to you as everything else."

Okay, that was a shot. "What the hell is that supposed to mean?"

"Oh, come on. No matter what you've done—saddle bronc riding, school, running the family business...you never break a sweat." Bryant leaned against the credenza, waving one hand at the bookcases on the opposite wall. The shelves groaned under the weight of ribbons, trophies and prized belt buckles the Murphy boys had earned over the years, the majority of them belonging to Liam. "You set your mind to accomplish something, and bam, you're first in your class."

The sarcasm in his brother's voice made Liam's blood boil. He was proud of what he'd accomplished as a professional cowboy, but he could care less about the display. Their dad had put that together when this office used to be his, long before Liam had taken over as president and CEO, and it remained now as a showpiece for potential clients.

Rising slowly to his feet, Liam noticed Nolan doing the same, but ignored him and turned his gaze on Bryant. "I sweated plenty, not to mention busted my ass, before I turned pro and every day after that when it came to riding."

"And in less than a year you were in the top five. Hell, the top two."

"Again, with plenty of blood, sweat and hard work." Liam was at a loss as to where his brother's resentment was coming from. He walked around the end of his desk, closing the distance between them. "You know that. You were there."

"Yeah, I was there at the University of Wyoming when you decided your rodeo career was over and college was the next step. Believe me, the campus wasn't that big and you cast a long shadow. You still do, Mr. President."

Liam shook his head.

It seemed that out of all of his brothers, Liam's relationship with Bryant had always been the most antagonistic over the years, despite his easy-going nature with everyone else. Adam and Nolan were typical older brothers, bossy and caretakers at the same time. He and Devlin, being born only eleven months apart, should have been competitive as well; instead they'd grown up close, but independent of each other.

Yeah, Liam had finally gone to college the same year as Bryant, but because he'd been twenty-one, he'd been allowed his own off-campus apartment. Liam had also carried a lot of anger over the twists and turns his life had taken at that point and had decided that it was best he lived alone, turning down his brother's offer to be roommates.

The two of them had graduated the same year and had come to work for the family business, but it'd been Liam who'd gone from sales manager to CEO in record time.

He'd always thought Bryant had been okay with that. Each family member was an equal shareholder in the company, and Liam's promotion wouldn't have happened without his brother's vote.

Besides, that had been years ago. His brother was still upset after all this time? "Are you saying you don't like the way I'm doing my job?"

"Guys…" Nolan's warning tone cut the air between them.

Bryant shook his head. "Forget it."

Liam took a step closer. "Like hell. First fatherhood and now this. What is going on with you?"

Bryant opened his mouth, but then Adam strolled into the room with his son, A.J., in his arms, cutting him off. "So this is where you're hiding out. Dad says to get a move on, he and the twins are drowning in all the estrogen out there. Personally, I think he loves being surrounded by the ladies—"

Adam paused then, his gaze quickly darting around the room, from brother to brother to brother. "Whoa, what's going on here?"

"We're trying to figure that out," Nolan said. "Without much success."

"Bryant's evidently got a stick up his butt about Casey—" Liam said, recalling how all this started.

"This has nothing to do with Casey." His brother cut him off, his tone quieter now, his gaze on his boots. "Not really."

Liam looked at Nolan and Adam, seeing that they were as confused as he was. He pulled in a deep breath and took a step back. "He seems to think life has handed me the world on a silver platter and finding out I'm a dad fifteen years too late is just going to be one more smooth ride for me."

"Well, you always were the smart one," Adam said. "Straight A's and barely cracking a book."

"The most popular and always got the girl," Nolan added. "And the best rides."

Yeah, until a horse had damn near taken his arm off and ended his dream. "Geesh, thanks, guys. I really feel the love."

"Hey, you're a hard worker, we all know that," Nolan said. "Even Bryant. But you always were a lucky SOB."

"You scored again with Casey. She's a sweetheart," Adam remarked.

"I know that," Liam snapped.

"But seeing how moony-eyed you've been over Missy the last couple of days, never mind the fact those two are only here temporarily," Adam continued, switching his son from one arm to the other, "I'd say things might not come quite so easy for you this time. In fact, unless I'm reading this situation all wrong, you could be in for the ride of your life."

Chapter Seven

Liam had been ready to tell his brothers what they could do with their opinions of his past and what he faced in the immediate future when it came to Missy and Casey, but then Nolan's twins had barreled into the office, insisting dinner was heading to the table.

The last one to walk into the dining room, he was still fired up over their simplistic view of his accomplishments. He'd worked damn hard for everything he'd ever gotten.

So what if he'd known from the age of ten that he wanted a rodeo career? Yes, he had a natural talent for staying in the saddle from the very beginning, but easy? Hell, it had been anything but, and making the choice to walk away from that dream had been the hardest thing he'd ever done.

Almost as hard as walking away from a future with Missy.

Thankfully his attention was diverted to the women emerging from the kitchen, in particular one beautiful blonde with sparkling blue eyes and a wide smile. She wore a simple sundress that left her arms bare and showed off her tiny waist, but what caught his eye was the way her hair hung in soft golden waves past her shoulders.

Missy laughed at something Fay and Laurie said, and the sweet sound caused the stiffness riding across his shoulders to diminish.

She followed his mother's lead and placed the heaping tray of fried chicken in the middle of the table alongside the rest of the meal. Then she looked up, her gaze moving around the room, across the crowd gathered there, as if searching for...

When she spotted him, the slight tilt of her head, the softening of her smile and the concern in her gaze were so familiar it took his breath.

Back in high school, before he'd summoned the courage to really talk to her, there'd been times when he'd caught her watching him—in class, across the lunch room, by the lockers in a crowded hallway—and a silent communication would pass between them. It had never lasted long, but in those moments, she'd made him feel...

Connected.

It was weird that he could now put a name to that strange feeling. Back then, he'd been cocky enough to think she was looking because he was one of the popular kids, or word had gotten out how well he'd done at a rodeo the weekend before.

After they'd started dating, he'd come to realize it was something else. Something he hadn't been able to describe. He'd never even tried, being a typical self-centered teenage boy.

Until he'd told her he loved her.

Missy looked away and took the seat in front of her.

Casey was next to her and she in turn was next to Luke; he'd wrestled with his twin for the spot.

Liam marched across the room, determined to take the empty chair on Missy's other side. He yanked the seat back, his elbow jostled with another and he looked up at Bryant, who was mirroring his actions for the empty chair next to his.

He froze, and the two of them stared at each other for a long moment.

"What's going on, you two?" Their father's booming voice carried from his place at the head of the table. "Sit so we can say grace."

When Laurie tugged at her husband's arm, Bryant looked away and Liam swore the man looked almost sick as he took his seat.

Liam sat down, thankful for the cold beer that appeared at his place setting. Eyeing Nolan across from him, he offered a quick salute to say thank-you before taking a long swallow.

His mother cleared her throat and Liam realized they were waiting on him. He put the beer down and then everyone bowed their heads. His father gave simple thanks for the people dining here tonight, the family members who weren't and the food before them, the familiar words binding the family together.

Then controlled chaos broke out as everyone started filling their plates and multiple conversations flowed around the table.

"Are you okay?" Missy's whispered question and the gentle nudge of her elbow against his caused Liam to tighten his grip on the platter he held. "You seem distracted."

"I'm fine." The words were automatic. Liam paused, realizing he meant them now that he was with her. He smiled and passed her the chicken without taking any. "Just a long day at the office."

"Don't you want some?" she asked, holding the dish back out to him.

"Ladies first."

Missy smiled, served herself and placed two large pieces on his plate as well. "You look like you've worked up an appetite."

The sudden image of the two of them doing just that flashed in his head.

Not a memory from long ago—fumbling beneath blankets, unsure of what exactly they were doing, but positive it was the right thing—but a vision of her stretched out across the white sheets of his bed, her hair flowing across his pillows as he moved over her—

"Hey, earth to Liam? Yo, man, you want some of this?"

Swearing softly beneath his breath, Liam pushed the fantasy to the back of his mind and took the large bowl of mashed potatoes Nolan offered. This time, he spooned a portion for himself, not wanting Missy to feel as if she needed to fill his plate.

"Would you like some?" he then asked her.

"Oh, no, thank you. None for me."

Before he could respond, Casey leaned forward, peering around Missy. "Oh, mash! I'll take that. Mum's not a big potato fan. Too many calories."

"You like them?" he asked, passing Casey the bowl, glad to see she didn't harbor the same belief. A quick glance at Missy's curves clearly stated she didn't have anything to worry about, either.

"Potatoes in any form are a slice of heaven," Casey said, grinning. "You ever had cottage pie? Minced beef and veggies topped with mashed potatoes. Yum! Our cook makes a smashing good one."

"You have a cook?" Abby spoke up from where she sat directly across from Casey. She then rolled her eyes. "Let me guess. There's a butler, too."

Casey's smile vanished. "Reynolds and Mrs. Mimi have been with us for years. They're terrific. As is Delaney, our maid."

"Casey."

Missy admonished her daughter, but Liam was more interested in the way Casey's eyes narrowed as she leaned forward, her voice a low whisper as she looked directly at Abby. "Guess what? I haven't made my own bed since I was five."

"Oh, that's not true," Missy said, adding a generous helping of green salad to her plate. "Delaney doesn't go anywhere near your room."

Abby's eyes widened and Casey's smile returned as she straightened and then held out the bowl of potatoes. "Mash, cuz?"

"No, thank you. Unlike some people, I try to eat healthy."

Casey shrugged, set the bowl on the table and reached for an ear of buttered corn. "Must be hard making sure you're spiffing in your pom-pom skirt."

Abby stabbed her fork at the salad that filled her plate. "Nathan thinks it's worth the effort."

"Now, I bet he looks cracking in those tight footballer pants." Casey heaved a dramatic sigh. "Wouldn't mind catching a sight of that."

Liam glanced at Missy, wondering if she was taking in this back-and-forth between the girls, but she was now chatting with Katie, who sat across from her, between Abby and Nolan.

"So, what did you two do today?" he asked her when Katie left the table to refill the pitchers of iced tea and lemonade. "I'd hoped to see you before now, but work kept me busy."

"Unpacked, mostly. As you know, our luggage was here when we got back from Adam's last night, but after hours on horseback I was too tired to tackle anything but soaking my sore muscles."

Missy lounging in that claw-footed tub was another mental picture that'd be haunting his dreams tonight. "Nice to know you're putting that antique bathtub to good use."

A light blush colored her cheeks. "Be nice," she whispered.

He grinned. "Anything else?"

"I did some sketching on a few pieces for a potential client while Casey explored the wonders of the American telly. I think she binged on vampires, zombies and police procedure shows."

"I would love to see your work. If you wouldn't mind showing me?"

The blush returned, but Missy looked pleased. "No, I wouldn't mind. In fact, you've already seen some of it. The dress I'm wearing now, in fact."

He allowed his gaze to travel over her again, appreciating the chance to do so. "You look beautiful."

"Thank you. It's one of my favorites."

"I wasn't talking about the dress." He adopted her low tone and leaned in close again, the familiar scent of summertime peaches teasing his nose. "And can I add how much I like finally seeing your hair down? I'd wondered if it was still as long as when I saw you last."

"Oh, goodness, no. I tend to wear it up and out of the way most days."

Liam started to tell her he hoped she wouldn't while staying here, but a noise drew Missy's attention to the far end of the table. He looked as well and found Fay trying to eat while balancing a fussy A.J. on her lap.

Seconds later, Adam noticed and reached for his son, easily cradling the baby's backside with one hand, gently bouncing him against his chest, never missing a beat with his own dinner.

Now there was a father for you.

Liam's eldest brother had taken to fatherhood the minute he found out Fay was pregnant, doing everything he could to make things easy for her, even moving Fay into his place after she'd had a health scare. And that was long before they'd admitted their feelings for each other and married. Even though A.J. was only six months old, Adam was already talking about adding to their family.

The sight of his brother placing a gentle kiss on his son's head as the baby snuggled into his shoulder had Liam suddenly thinking about what it would've felt like to hold Casey like that back when she was that age.

Had she been a fussy baby or more like A.J., who was a happy kid most of the time? Had Missy's husband held her in his arms, soothing her? Had Casey found the same contentment that Adam's son seemed to, with his tiny fist grabbing hold of his dad's shirt?

A sharp sting bit at Liam's eyes and he turned away only to find Missy watching him again, an unreadable expression in her gaze.

"Ah, sh—shoot."

The sound of glass hitting the table came from Liam's other side and he turned in time to see Bryant had up-ended the whiskey tumbler he'd brought with him from Liam's office.

Liam reached for the mess with his napkin at the same time Bryant did.

"I got it, I got it," he said, pushing Liam's hands away

as he mopped up the liquid. "Probably should've stopped at one."

"Yeah, probably."

Bryant's gaze held fire. "You know, you've got—"

"Honey, please." Laurie reached over and laced her fingers with his, stopping whatever he planned to say. "Let's do this."

"You sure?" His tone softened and he brought the back of her hand to his mouth for a quick kiss. "I thought you might want to wait...longer."

She shook her head, lightly cleared her throat and then said, "Hey, everyone. Could we get your attention?"

Silence filled the air.

Laurie smiled, and then looked at Bryant. "Go ahead."

"Well, we asked the folks to pull this dinner together tonight because we have some news to share." Bryant gave his wife's hand a squeeze and gazed into her eyes. "Great news. We're going to have a baby."

And in that instant, his brother's earlier ramblings made sense to Liam.

Happy cries filled the room, led by their mother, who jumped up from her seat to give Laurie and Bryant each a hug and a kiss, followed by their father, who'd also left his place to congratulate the happy couple. Hugs, handshakes and high fives were exchanged and Liam threw his arm around his brother's shoulder, giving him a hearty slap on the back.

"Oh, maybe we'll have another girl in the family and then we'll be even," Elise said, taking her seat again, wiping at her eyes with her napkin. "Three boys and three girls, now that Casey has joined us. For so long Abby was the only granddaughter."

"All the better."

Liam glanced sharply at Casey, wondering if she'd

heard Abby's mumbled words, but with her head bowed, she seemed intently focused on her meal. Where was his niece's animosity coming from anyway?

"So when do we get to meet my newest grandchild?" Alistair asked.

"The end of January," Laurie said.

Liam started counting, but his father was faster. "So, that makes you four months along."

Laurie nodded, her fingers shaking as she tucked a strand of hair behind one ear. "We wanted to wait...well, until..."

Bryant reached for his wife's hand again. "After the miscarriage last year, we thought it would be best if we waited until Laurie was out of her first trimester before we shared the news."

"Makes sense," Liam said, remembering that during Laurie's first pregnancy his brother had shared they'd been trying to start a family since their honeymoon a few years ago. The loss of their child and Laurie's health issues since had hit Bryant hard.

When everyone started chatting again, he leaned in toward his brother and lowered his voice. "So does our talk earlier in my office."

"I'm a jerk." Bryant's mouth rose into a sheepish grin.

"You're a Murphy. It happens sometimes." Liam smiled. "And like the rest of the Murphy men, you're going to be a great father."

"Thanks. So are you, man."

Liam hoped his brother was right.

Despite Missy's assurances and his own common sense telling him it was too soon, he didn't feel much like one at the moment. He and Casey were polite strangers, almost friends, maybe. That was a long way from what his brothers shared with their children.

"Go on, Fay, it's okay." Laurie's words cut into his thoughts and he found his sisters-in-law sharing smiles from across the table.

"Oh, no," Fay said, her curls bouncing as she shook her head. "I don't want to spoil your news."

"You couldn't. Go on."

"But I haven't even told Adam yet."

"So tell him now."

"Tell me what now?" Adam asked, looking at his wife. "What secret are you two sharing?"

"Okay, then." Fay smiled, her gaze moving around the table before it landed on her husband. "Well, I'm afraid the male/female grandkid ratio will still be uneven next year, because I'm pregnant, too."

Adam's mouth fell open, a stunned expression on his face before he gave out a loud whoop and gathered his wife and son in his arms.

More cheers and hugs were passed around by everyone.

When Fay shared she was due only a couple of weeks after Laurie, the remainder of the meal was filled with talk of baby showers, ideas for names and Logan and Luke insisting that another set of twins in the family would be the coolest thing ever, even if their uncles paled at that suggestion.

It wasn't until the table was cleared and his mother put her able-bodied grandkids in charge of kitchen cleanup and then served dessert, that Liam realized Missy was no longer in the room.

She needed a moment.

Walking out on a family celebration was rude. Missy's well-mannered upbringing haunted her with every step, but the love and happiness overflowing in the dining room had been vastly dissimilar from her own experience. And right now it was more than she could handle.

The air was warm here on the front porch, despite it being a cloudy day. Distant rumblings coming from the dark skies overhead promised rain was on its way. A rich scent of earth and grass and trees filled her head, so unlike what she was used to at home, but familiar again after being back here for the last few days.

Seeking peace and quiet to gather her thoughts, Missy made her way to the seating area where she and Liam had talked that first night. Then she would go back inside. She'd rejoin the others and smile and be happy for them because deep in her heart, she truly felt the news of a baby's—or babies'—arrival was wonderful.

But first she needed to deal with the memory of her family's reaction when she'd finally found the courage to tell them...

Oh, it had been far different.

Crossing her arms, Missy lifted her face to the light breeze, her eyes closed in an attempt to hold back the tears.

Even after all this time, she could still hear the distress in their voices, see the disapproval in their eyes as she stood before them in her father's study and confessed she was pregnant and even worse, didn't know who the baby's father was.

"Missy, are you all right?"

Liam calling out caused her to jump, and she hastily brushed at the wetness on her cheeks, erasing the tears that managed to escape despite her best efforts.

"Sorry, didn't mean to startle you," he said as he came closer. "It's just that you left so abruptly—"

"I'm the one who should apologize." She cut him off as she turned around with a pasted-on smile and a determination not to let him see the turmoil crashing around inside her. "It just got too warm—too many people—"

"What's wrong?" His eyes narrowed as he looked at her. "Why are you upset?"

"I'm not. Not really." Surprised at how easily the lie fell from her lips, she quickly dropped her gaze from his. "You come bearing gifts."

Liam held a dessert plate with two forks in the same hand. "It's one of my mother's specialties. Her blue-ribbon-winning apple pie, complete with a heaping scoop of vanilla ice cream."

"So very American." Happy for the distraction, Missy reached for the plate, but Liam stepped back, holding the treat out of reach. "You don't plan to share?" she asked.

"Of course I do. As soon as you share what's bothering you."

"I told you—"

"If anyone knows how overwhelming my family can be at times, it's me," Liam said, putting the dessert on a nearby table. "But I get the feeling it's something more. Somehow related to the happy news?"

"I think your sisters-in-law being pregnant at the same time is jolly wonderful." Missy kept her gaze low. "For them, for your brothers, for everyone."

Bending his knees a bit, he scrunched down, trying to bring his face level with hers. When that didn't work, he gently lifted her chin with his finger and forced her to look at him. "And the family's reaction to that news was nothing like what you received sixteen years ago."

She closed her eyes and turned away to look out over the yard, not surprised he had figured out the cause of her distress so easily. He'd always been able to read her.

"No, it wasn't," she finally admitted.

"Tell me."

A shuddering breath escaped her lungs and she shook her head.

"Please." He moved in behind her, so close she could almost feel his warmth. His strength. Then his hands encircled her upper arms, his touch causing a shiver to dance across her skin. "I'd like to know."

"There's not much to tell." She pulled in a deep breath and slowly exhaled. "Picture the exact opposite reaction. My father, sitting in his chair by the fireplace, remaining stoic, even as his eyes raked over me with censure and condemnation."

"Aw, Missy…"

"Believe it or not, that was easier to take than my mother, who didn't even look at me. No, she just cried out and then dropped her crystal sherry glass, shattering it into a million pieces."

"You were alone? That bastard didn't even stand next to you—"

How had he guessed that? "I told Stanford I wanted… needed to speak to them by myself. To explain."

A long silence filled the air before Liam said, "Because you didn't know if the baby was his or mine."

Missy dropped her chin, amazed that the memory of that night still lived so fresh in her mind. That it still hurt so much.

"They, of course, assumed the baby was Stanford's, but then I told them about falling in lo—" She bit hard on her bottom lip, cutting off her words for a moment. "About meeting you. About what happened when I first returned home to London. Why it took me so long to realize…"

"What did they say?"

"Nothing. I was sent to my room. They didn't speak to me for three days."

His hands tightened on her. "That's kind of harsh."

"I'd shocked them, shocked their neat and orderly world. Now, as an adult, I can understand that. My time in America changed me. I was more independent, more vocal in my opinions. At eighteen, I was technically an adult, but in their eyes, I was still a child. Their only child."

She turned to face him, breaking free of his hold. "Oh, this is silly. I don't know why I'm letting this bother me now. It's a totally different situation. Fay and Laurie are grown women, happily married. Of course the reactions would be different."

Liam's brows drew together in a scowl. "That's still no reason for your parents to treat you that way."

"How do you think Nolan would react if Abby came home one day and shared that kind of news? How would I if Casey ever does the same?"

He looked as thunderstruck as she felt, and he backed away, rubbing his hand hard across his mouth. "You wouldn't shut her out," he said. "You wouldn't ignore her and then find a way to manipulate the situation to suit your own needs."

The strength and sureness in his words warmed her. "Thank you for saying that."

"I wish I had known." He came back to her, his hands cupping her face, his thumbs gently brushing against her damp cheeks. "I wish you had told me you were pregnant. That the child might be mine."

"Oh, Liam...what would you have done?"

"I don't know. Flown to England?"

She tried to shake her head at the absurdity of his words, but he held her in place, his eyes boring into hers. "I would've found a way to be with you. To support you until we knew for sure—"

"And then what? My father obviously planned all along to lie about the test results when the time came."

He closed his eyes, a pained expression on his face.

Without thinking, without considering the consequences, she gave in to the need to touch him. Her fingertips scraped the roughness of his evening beard as she touched his jaw.

"After Casey was born, you would've been told the same thing I had...that she wasn't yours," she whispered, her throat tightening as the imagined scene played out in her mind. "And I would've lost you all over again. I don't know if I could've lived through that a second time—"

His mouth crashed down on hers, his kiss raw and unapologetic as he devoured her confession, his tongue sweeping inside.

It was as surprising as when he'd kissed her the other night, but this time she didn't pull away. This time their mouths pushed and queried, relearning, remembering, and when a low groan filled the air, she didn't know if it came from him or her.

The hint of apple and cinnamon on his tongue tasted sweet, the dark sweeping heat of it stroking hers almost savage. His fingers pressed hard against her jaw and then he released her.

She stumbled forward, her breasts brushing against his chest, and his grip returned as the kiss continued. He pulled her toward him until she was flush against his body. She scraped her fingers over his jaw to his hair, her arms sliding up and over his shoulders until they intertwined behind his neck.

The past and present meshed and mingled; she was a girl again in the arms of her first love, her first lover. At the same time his kiss, his touch, his body were new to her in so many ways, and a desire to know him, to be with the man he was now, raced through her.

The kiss seemed to go on forever, a rising desire that

threatened to consume her, consume both of them, until she finally broke free, light-headed and breathless, sure her legs wouldn't keep her upright if he weren't holding her so tightly.

"Liam…"

He pulled her even closer, his arms banding around her as he tucked her head to his shoulder, his face buried into her neck. His lips grazed her skin, his breaths heavy and warm as he whispered in her ear. "Just let me hold you… for a moment."

Knowing she couldn't refuse him—and didn't want to—she relaxed into his embrace and allowed her eyelids to close, the fleeting glimpse of a figure standing in the shadows near the doorway registering in her mind.

Missy gasped and opened her eyes, pushing at Liam's shoulders. He let her go and stepped back, confusion crossing his features.

"Missy—"

"Someone is…" Her words came in a hushed whisper. "Watching us."

"With a family as big as mine, I'm not surprised." He squeezed her hand tightly, his smile unsteady. "This isn't the most private place to talk…or do anything else."

"You don't bloody understand." Panic raced through her veins and she yanked free and stepped away, the cool air now swirling between them. "I think it was Casey."

Chapter Eight

Missy had, as the Americans so often put it, chickened out when it came to asking Casey if she'd been the one who'd seen her and Liam talking—and kissing—out on the front porch a few nights ago.

She'd expected her daughter to come right out and demand an explanation, if not in front of everyone at least with her privately, when she and Liam had sneaked back inside, but the group's attention had been on the large-screen television where old family movies were playing as they ate dessert.

Casey had been sitting next to Liam's mother, watching the telly and listening to Elise's stories about the boys when they were young. Missy had started to go to her when Liam grabbed her hand and pulled her down next to him on a nearby love seat.

After practically landing in his lap, she'd managed to scoot to the far side of the diminutive sofa, shoving a couple of toss pillows between the two of them before Casey turned and sent a big smile her way.

Later, when the evening had ended and the two of them headed back to the boathouse, she'd waited, but again nothing. Deciding it might have been one of his brothers after all, Missy had remained silent on the subject.

In the days since, the three of them had settled into a routine where she and Casey occupied themselves in the morning, but then Liam would join them for lunch at the main house before he went back to his office. Afternoons were spent either poolside or off doing something with Liam's mother, including today, when they had gone to Cheyenne and done touristy stuff with the twins tagging along.

And as much as Missy tried not to impose, Elise insisted they eat dinner at the main house with her and her husband every night. Liam was there, too, of course. More often than not Nolan and his kids joined them, even though at times Abby didn't seem too pleased to have Missy and Casey at the table.

Not that the teen said anything directly to her, but Missy had picked up on the verbal jabs she and Casey tossed back and forth, usually under their breath and the radar of everyone else.

Missy had mentioned it to her daughter the first night it happened as they were heading to bed, but Casey had laughed it off as "not a bloody big deal."

The evenings were nice, filled with watching movies, playing board games—Casey was as cutthroat at Monopoly as Liam—or spending time outside, either taking long walks, being lakeside on the dock or sitting around a fire.

The three of them were always together and often joined by others. Meaning Missy and Liam weren't ever alone.

She'd told him on that first night there would be nothing between them, no rekindling of a long-ago flame. Missy had decided the best way to ensure that was to keep the focus of their time together on Casey, allowing her and Liam to get to know one another. Again, it was something Liam was being a perfect gentleman about.

Oh, she would catch him sending slow, appraising looks her way, his gaze not giving away what was going on inside his head. But then his hand would brush against hers during a meal, or land warm and strong at the small of her back when they walked, sending an all too familiar tingling through her.

But that was as far as it went. It was as if they'd reached an unspoken agreement of what was important. And what wasn't.

After Missy and Casey had spent today shopping and sightseeing with Liam's mother and the twins, Casey had received a text from Liam asking if they were going to make it back in time for dinner. They arrived at the main house in the late afternoon, the twins jumping from their grandmother's car to sprint across the yard toward their own home.

"Where are they off to?" Elise asked.

"Something about who can win a race to the loo," Casey said with a grin. "Uh, to the bathroom, I mean."

Elise laughed. "I guess it's a good thing they have more than one. Come on, let's go inside."

"We ought to take these back to the boathouse," Missy said, lifting the bags filled with the clothes and trinkets she and Casey had managed to accumulate during today's outing from Elise's car. "Perhaps what we should have purchased was another suitcase—"

The tooting of a horn had all three of them turning around.

It was Fay in her pretty personalized van for her flower shop. She parked in an empty space and waved at them through the open window. "Hello there! I come bearing flowers and a baby. You do remember what tonight is?"

"Of course I do," Elise said, and then turned to Missy as they walked toward the van. "She and Adam have standing date nights the second and last Friday of every month. If I'm real lucky, I get to keep my handsome grandson with us overnight."

Missy smiled at Elise's enthusiasm, surprised that August was almost over. She and Casey had been in Destiny a week today and it'd been almost a month since her father died.

And their world had turned upside down.

"Missy, can I ask you a favor?" Fay asked, opening the side door and reaching for her son's car carrier in the backseat. "Would you mind taking this guy into the house and keeping an eye on him for a few minutes? Elise and I have to get the flower arrangements for the model homes."

"Of course I don't mind." Handing off their bags to Casey, Missy looked down at A.J. He was waving his fists in the air, his eyes scrunched up tight against the afternoon sunshine. "Hey, there, buddy. You seem a bit cranky."

"He just woke up from a nap and will probably want a bottle. Don't worry, he can wait until I get into the house."

Missy took the baby's nappy bag from Fay, slinging the strap over one shoulder, the gesture familiar, despite the passage of time. "I think I remember how it's done, if you trust me. Do you have a bottle made up already?"

"Great, go for it." Fay grinned and handed over her son. "The bottles are in the side pocket and Elise has an electronic warmer on the counter. Just pop one in, wait for the ready light and you're good to go."

"Katie's car is still in the lot and the boys should be nearby if you need help," Elise said from the back of the van, where she'd opened the rear double doors. "Oh, Fay, these flowers are gorgeous. Perfect for the coming fall season."

"I was hoping you'd like them," Fay said, and then looked to Missy again. "If you need me, just give a shout."

"We'll be fine," Missy said, hefting the baby's carrier into the crook of her arm. "I've got all the help I need right here."

"Who, me?" Casey's eyes grew wide as she backed away, holding her hands loaded with bags up in mock surrender. "I don't know nothin' 'bout birthin' babies!"

Everyone laughed at her spot-on high-pitched imitation from one of the two classic films they'd watched last night.

"Birthin' and babysitting are two different things." The memory of what she'd said to Liam a few nights ago flashed in Missy's head, but she pushed it away and smiled at her daughter. "Don't worry. I'll talk you through it."

Elise and Fay got to work with the flowers while Missy and Casey headed for the side door that took them directly into the living room.

Missy stopped at one of the leather sofas in the main seating area in front of the fireplace and set A.J.'s carrier on the floor. She easily found a bottle in the baby's bag. "Keep an eye on the little bugger while I warm this up, okay?"

"You better make it fast." Casey stared at the baby with a dubious glare. "With the faces he's making it looks like he's about to go off his trolley."

Bending down, Missy touched the soft brown curls on the baby's head. His dark eyes latched onto the bottle in her hand.

She quickly straightened and tucked his afternoon treat behind her back, but it was too late. "I think you're right. I'll be back in a moment."

Casey dropped the shopping bags on the couch and sat. "So, what do I do in the meantime?"

"Distract him. Try chatting him up," Missy said, heading for the kitchen.

Finding the warming device, she followed the easy directions, wishing she'd had one of these years ago. Hmm, four to six minutes before mealtime. She peeked back into the main room as the baby's fussing got louder. The last thing she wanted was to bother anyone in the nearby offices or send Casey to get his mother.

"Nudge the carrier gently with your foot, sweetie," she suggested, calling out her daughter. "The rocking motion might calm him down. It's going to take a few minutes before his bottle is ready."

Casey rolled her eyes, but stretched out one foot, the tip of her cowboy boot catching the hard plastic edge of the carrier and setting it into motion. "You know, I'm a bit parched myself."

Missy smiled and then went to work preparing a tray of chocolate-chip cookies and lemonade, not wanting to spoil their appetites.

The moment she heard the clear and pure tone of her daughter's voice raised in song, she froze.

Making her way back to the doorway, she found Casey still rocking the baby's seat with her foot, but she also now had a guitar in her arms as she sang a favorite song of hers about blue skies, wishing on a star and bluebirds flying over a rainbow.

A warm feeling of pride filled Missy, her heart pounding so hard she had to press a hand to her chest.

Music was one of her daughter's passions. A day rarely went by when she wasn't singing or playing. Missy had meant to check with Liam about the piano against the far wall after noticing Casey glancing at it a few times.

She had no idea where her daughter had found the instrument she was playing now. It looked a little beat-up, much like the one Casey had back home that she'd bought last year, after spotting it in the window of a secondhand shop on Rathbone Place.

Could it be— No, she doubted Liam would still have that old thing.

The last rich, mellow notes of the simple melody lingered in the air as Casey finished and smiled down at the baby. "So, A.J., you're a music fan. I like that. Bollocks, don't start fussing again."

A.J. wasn't listening as his soft whimpers started to rise in volume.

"That was beautiful," said a male voice. "Maybe you should try singing to him again."

Casey whipped her head around when Liam spoke. Missy did the same, her wide eyes matching their daughter's startled expression.

At finding him there, Liam guessed, but he'd been the one who was truly surprised.

He'd been ending a phone call when Katie popped into his office, letting him know his mother's car had just pulled into the driveway. Missy and Casey were back. A sudden need to see them had hit him square in the chest and he realized he'd missed them.

Ever since that night on the front porch, Missy had been finding creative ways to stay away from him, or at least ensure they weren't alone again. He could admit he'd gotten a bit carried away with that kiss, but her story—and his frustration over a past they couldn't change—had hit him harder than he'd expected.

Shaking off the memory, Liam decided to concentrate on what was happening now between them. As much as he claimed it was all about him and Casey getting to know each other, he knew there was more to it.

More to him and Missy.

Unfinished business? Something new?

He didn't have any idea. But he was eager to share something he'd come up with today, something he hoped Casey would be excited about.

Something that might give him more one-on-one time with Missy.

"Go on," Liam urged when Casey continued to stare at him while the baby's fussing grew louder. He walked to the sofa opposite where Casey sat, fisting his hands along the back cushions. "He looks like he's about to burst into a joyful noise. Something I'm sure won't sound anywhere near as terrific as you."

Casey's cheeks turned bright pink at his compliment. She dropped her chin and looked away, but the shy smile visible on her face warmed Liam's heart.

She then pulled in a deep breath, slowly released it and started the song again. Her grip on the instrument looked steady as her fingers moved over the strings with a familiar ease. Her voice was solid and unwavering this time as she looked again at her baby cousin, who'd gone silent as soon as she began to sing.

Damn, she was good.

It was obvious she had a natural gift and some training. Much more than Liam. He'd learned to play some when he was a kid from an old cowboy turned logger who used to work for the family business. The rest he'd picked up on his own.

Glancing over his shoulder, he found that Katie and Nolan had followed him and were enjoying the impromptu concert. He then looked across the room and saw that his mom and Fay had come in as well, but it was the delight on Missy's face as she looked at Casey that caused a hard lump to form in his throat.

This obviously wasn't the first time she'd heard their daughter sing.

When had Casey started? Was this something new or had she begun at a much younger age? Then he wondered if someone in her life had discovered and nurtured this talent or if it had come naturally.

Perhaps it was inherited from him?

Damn. How much had he missed out on during the years he hadn't known about his daughter?

He wondered too how she'd known his guitars were kept in a nearby cabinet. He still played every once in a while, and a sudden eagerness to share this moment had him crossing the room and reaching for the second guitar leaning against a low shelf.

He slipped the strap over his head and easily picked up the melody she was playing as he returned to sit on the empty sofa.

She stopped mid-chorus, but Liam nodded for her to continue. Casey returned his nod and moved on to the next line of lyrics without missing a beat, her smile and the slight uptick of her chin an invitation for him to join in. He did, keeping his baritone range low, melding it easily with her sweet soprano, before backing off completely when she softened her tone on the last line, her fingertips drawing out the ending cords.

A light clapping filled the air as A.J. slapped his chubby hands together and gurgled happily.

Liam and Casey laughed; the thrill of achieving an eight-second ride on the back of a bucking bronc paled in comparison to the happiness slamming in his gut at this very moment.

More applause came, this time from everyone else as

they moved farther into the room, gathering around the seating area.

"Oh, sweetie, that was wonderful," Elise gushed.

"What an amazing voice you have," Katie added. "I love your version of that song."

Fay knelt next to her son, unstrapping him from his car seat and lifting him into her arms. "You do realize you've spoiled this young man," she said, giving Casey a smile. "He's never going to be happy with my sorry attempts at bedtime lullabies again."

Missy handed Fay the warmed bottle once she settled onto the sofa, and then she came and sat next to Casey. "That was smashing. I've missed hearing you while I was gone." Then she looked over at him. "It's nice to know you still play, too."

Liam smiled, remembering how he used to serenade her during those stolen hours in the boathouse attic. He'd managed to learn a favorite song of hers, a popular country tune at the time. He was no Tim McGraw, but he'd managed to sing to her about what her love did to him.

And how she made him who he wanted to be.

"Yeah, he still entertains the family from time to time," Nolan said, reaching over and lightly punching Liam on the shoulder. "You two should get together with Abby and do a—"

"Do a what?" Abby asked, interrupting her father as she strolled into the room with Luke and Logan right behind her. "What's going on?"

"Casey and Liam just sang a duet," Fay said. "A lullaby for A.J."

"Oh, really?" Abby walked to the piano and perched on the short end of the bench, one hand lightly running across a few of the keys, the clear notes filling the air. "How sweet."

"She's great," Katie said. "You really missed something."

"I'm sure I did."

Liam studied his niece. Something was bothering her. There was a stiffness in her posture, an indifference that set off his radar. Before he could say anything, Casey spoke up.

"Do you sing?" she asked, directing her question to Abby.

"Are you kidding? She sounds like a bullfrog in heat."

"Logan." Nolan shot his son a warning look. "Knock it off."

"No, I play." Abby turned and faced the piano. Using both hands this time, she played a quick classical piece with precision, ending with a flourish before looking back over her shoulder. "In fact, Uncle Liam and I play together all the time. We're the musical ones in the family."

"I can see that." Casey's voice was flat as she placed the guitar on the sofa next to her and got to her feet. "Well, I better tote our bags to the boathouse."

Liam blinked; the quicksilver change in Casey's demeanor surprised him. Gone was the beaming girl he'd just had an incredible moment with. In fact, her face was wiped clean of any emotion at all.

Missy reached out, placing a hand on her daughter's arm before the girl could grab the first bag. "Casey, what's wro—uh, I thought you wanted something to drink."

"I'll get something for all of us," Elise said. "Katie, would you like to help me?"

The two women disappeared into the kitchen, but Liam was more interested in the abrupt tension in the air, not to mention the nonverbal conversation going on between mother and daughter.

Casey stared at Missy for a long moment, blew out a dramatic puff of air and flopped back to the couch. "Fine."

Missy grabbed for the guitar before it toppled to the rug, handing it to Liam. "Here, you might want to put this away for safekeeping."

"But I thought she might—" His gaze moved from her to Casey. "I thought you might like to keep it. Take it back to the apartment with you."

Casey shrugged, not looking at him, her focus now on the silver rings decorating her fingers. "I know where it is if I want to play again."

"How did you know where to find these in the first place?" he asked.

"I noticed the door to the cabinet was open and spotted the buggers." She finally looked at him again. "Why? Can't I touch them?"

The chill of her tone surprised him. "Of course you can."

"Hey, you never let us play with them," Luke said.

"Because they aren't toys." Liam softened the words with a smile. "Casey knows how to play, quite well, I might add. If I were to guess, I'd say she also knows how to take care of guitars because she has one of her own?"

The hardness eased from her eyes. "It's nothing special. A secondhand Cordoba C5."

Liam nodded. "Nice. These are both Fenders, not new by any stretch, but they do hold value to me, especially sentimental. And you're free to use either one. Any time you want. Any place you'd like."

A flicker of a smile returned to Casey's face as his mom and Katie came back into the room with a tray of glasses, pitchers of iced tea and lemonade, and a large platter of homemade cookies that the twins immediately dug into.

Picking up both guitars, Liam returned them to the cabinet and then took his seat again, noticing Casey's gaze following his every move.

"So what are everyone's plans for dinner?" Elise asked. "I know Fay is heading home for her date with Adam, but who's interested in homemade pizzas?"

The twins' hands shot up, Nolan's, too, but it was the shared glance between Missy and Casey that had Liam speaking up. "None for us, Mom," he said. "I thought I'd take these two ladies to the Blue Creek Saloon tonight."

Casey's eyes sparkled with life again. "Really? We can eat at that place that was once a real Old West saloon?"

"Sure." Liam caught Missy's eye. "Don't worry. It's changed from the rowdy bar you might remember. Well, somewhat. It doesn't get crazy there on Friday nights until later. It's very much a family restaurant. At least until the band kicks in."

"Band? They have live music? That's dench!"

Liam laughed, glad to see Casey's good mood was back. "I take it that's a good thing."

Casey nodded. "A cracking good thing. Let's go!"

"I think we should take our purchases back to the flat first. I'd also like to grab a shower and change," Missy said. "If that would be all right."

Liam nodded, fighting off the urge to picture her doing both of those things in vivid detail. It took a moment, but he got his head back on straight and held out his hand when they started to rise. "Before you go, there's something else I'd like to talk to Casey about."

"Can't we chat over dinner?" Casey asked.

"Well, sure, but this includes Nolan." Liam looked at his brother. "At least partially."

Casey's gaze flickered to Nolan for a moment, then to Abby, who'd left the piano to perch on the arm of the chair where her father sat, before coming back to Liam.

She shrugged. "Okay. What's up?"

A sliver of caution sliced through his chest as he looked at the curious expressions around the room. Hell, maybe he should have waited until they were alone to bring this up. Too late now.

"I want you to know I'm really happy you and your mother still have a few weeks in Destiny with me—with all of us—but I'm worried you might find your days…boring, especially after next week, when Abby and the twins head back to school."

"Man, don't remind us," Luke said.

"Yeah," Logan agreed. "Back to having tons of homework coming out our as—ah, ears."

Casey smiled at that and Liam took that as a good sign. "So, I thought maybe we could get you permission to attend classes at the high school," he continued. "To let you see what life is like at an American school, which I'm guessing is somewhat different than the private all-girls academy you go to."

"Is that possible?" Missy asked.

"Well, we've got an inside track." Liam glanced at his brother. "Nolan's been dating the vice principal for the last month, so I thought he could talk—"

"What!"

Abby's outcry and the jarring clunk of a glass against wood cut Liam off midsentence. He—and everyone else—looked first at Abby and then at Katie, who'd righted her drinking glass but was hastily wiping at the spill she'd caused on the large hand-hewn coffee table with a handful of napkins.

"Oh, I'm sorry. I didn't—" Katie jumped to her feet, tossing the wet mess onto the tray. "How clumsy of me. I'll just take this into the kitchen. Please, don't let me interrupt…your plans."

Katie hurried from the room, tray in hand, but Abby wasn't finished.

"Dad, you can't be getting serious with Ms. Elan," she cried, jumping to her feet. "Just because she won you at that silly bachelor auction? And as for her going to the high school—" Abby waved a hand in Casey's direction "—forget it! She was bragging the other night how she has nothing to do but laze around because she's on a holiday!"

"Hey, back up a minute." Nolan pointed at his daughter. "I've been out with MaryAnn twice since the auction date. That's hardly getting serious. And what Casey does or doesn't do during her stay isn't your call."

"Oh, she doesn't have to get her knickers in a twist." Casey stood as well. The anger flashing in her eyes as she glared at Abby told Liam his idea was shot all to hell. "I'd rather be bloody bored out of my skull than go to the same school as her. And I'm quite sure the feeling is mutual."

Chapter Nine

Trying to find a spot for a moment of privacy wasn't easy around here. Casey could only stay holed up in her room for so long. Thankfully everyone seemed occupied on Sunday afternoon, including her mum and Liam, who both had work-related issues to deal with, so she'd grabbed an apple, bottled water and her journal, thinking maybe she'd find some solitude here in the boathouse to put her jumbled thoughts down on paper.

She thought back to the night Liam and she had played guitar together. She'd been tempted all weekend to grab one. Then she'd spotted that piano and remembered what Abby had said to ruin the moment.

Trying to find common ground with Liam wasn't as easy as she'd thought it'd be.

The horseback riding had been fun, something she'd never been interested in despite her grandmother's attempts at getting her into lessons. But finding out that her real father was a former champion cowboy had changed that. And she was good at it. Liam had come right out and told her so.

Still, the moment he'd picked up that second guitar and started playing alongside her...

That simple act had caused a rush of powerful emotions. Then when their voices had blended in almost perfect harmony, all those crazy bounding sensations had boiled down to a simple longing she'd never felt before.

Longing to be connected.

It was the same—and yet different—feeling that she had toward her mum. The bond between them was as natural to her as breathing. But for the first time Casey had felt a link, even if it was fragile, between her and the man who was her real father.

Until that blonde prig had come along and ruined everything.

Not wanting to relive that memory again, Casey stepped out of the sunshine and into the cool, shadowy interior of the lower level of the boathouse, drawn by the sounds of the lake gently lapping against the boat slips.

Pushing her sunglasses to the top of her head, she looked around, debating if it'd be okay if she curled up on the bench seat of the wooden powerboat that sat bobbing in the first slip. It wasn't as if she planned to power that baby up—

"We've got plenty of kayaks, singles and doubles, not to mention a few—what are *you* doing in here?"

Casey whirled around. Blimey, just what she didn't need. Abby stood just inside the arched opening of the boathouse near the first slip, surrounded by a half dozen hangers-on this time.

The princess and her minions. Geesh, did they multiply?

"Looking for a little peace and quiet, but I guess that's

a bust." She hiked her drawstring bag higher on her shoulder. "Don't worry. I'll get out of your way."

"Good." Abby's voice dropped away, but she wasn't done. *You're not wanted*, she added, mouthing the words silently.

Biting her tongue because it just wasn't worth it, Casey settled for an old-fashioned eye roll as she brushed past her cousin, refusing to back down when Abby didn't move aside. Her minions scattered, so there was some satisfaction in that.

"Hey, Casey. I was just thinking about you. What are you doing?"

Her footsteps faltered and she looked up into familiar green eyes, but even the appearance of that good-looking lad she'd met last week couldn't save this moment.

"Leaving," she said.

"Wait." Nathan reached for her as she started past him, gently grabbing at her elbow. "Don't go. Stick around. Hang with us."

Casey stared at him. She could almost hear her cousin's head exploding behind her at the invitation. "No, I don't want to get in the way."

"You won't. Right, guys?"

Nathan let go of her and looked at his buddies, who all either nodded or shrugged with indifference as they walked past her and deeper into the boathouse.

Casey made a quick count. Seven lads, including Nathan, and six girls, not counting her. She wouldn't be the odd one out this time. At least not numerically. And she did have a good time when they all hung out at the pool, as long as she kept blinders on where her cousin was concerned.

Still, she wasn't sure—

"Don't tell me you can't swim?"

Nathan's question pulled her from her thoughts. "What? No, of course, I can swim." Casey looked over to where the crowd was putting kayaks in the water, slipping into the seats and heading out into the sunshine. "I've just never done that before."

"Oh, that's too bad." Abby called out in a false voice from where she sat on the edge of the dock, holding a double kayak in place with her feet. "All we seem to have left are singles."

Meaning Nathan was going to be getting into hers.

Casey gave what she hoped was a casual shrug. "Maybe next time."

"What next time?" Nathan walked backward toward the boat slips with a cocky grin. "You and I can take one of the rowboats. How about this blue one?"

Abby's eyes grew wide as she got to her feet. "Nate, wait."

"Don't worry, Abs, I can handle getting this thing off the storage rack—hey, what's this doing in here?"

Liam's guitar! Casey couldn't believe Nathan had it. Her gaze flew to Abby, catching the fleeting guilt in her eyes before it disappeared. She'd done it! Abby had taken one of Liam's prized possessions and hid it out here—for what?

Everyone had heard his offer that Casey could use one any time she wanted. Had Abby hoped someone would notice it missing and assume Casey had taken it without asking? Or worse, that the instrument would get damaged and she'd be blamed?

"I brought it." The words popped out of Casey's mouth before she could stop them. She had no idea why. She walked to Nathan and took the guitar from him, grateful to find it unharmed. "I was looking for a quiet spot to practice."

"You play?" he asked, easily maneuvering the rowboat

into the water and tying it to the slip. "Cool. Maybe you can serenade me once we get out on the water."

Casey turned and narrowed her gaze at her cousin. "Maybe. But I wouldn't want to get distracted and fall in. You might have to rescue me."

Abby returned her look for a moment, and then wheeled her attention back to the kayak, calling out to one of the other lads, who quickly abandoned his single to join her.

Casey looked back to Nathan, wondering if seeing Abby with someone else would bother him. No matter how fun it was to tease the priss—who didn't deserve any leeway after the stunt she'd just pulled—the last thing Casey wanted was to get in the middle of a teenage romance.

Been there, done that, never again.

"Don't worry, you're safe with me," Nathan said, grabbing a couple of life vests from a nearby shelf. "I spent the summer working at the local kids' camp as a lifeguard. But to be safe, let's put these on."

"Do you mind if I run upstairs and put these things away first?" Wow, did she sound like a breathless twit. "I mean, I trust you to save me, but I wouldn't want anything to happen to the guitar."

"Sure, I'll wait right here."

Casey gathered her things and started to walk around him when he stopped her. "Hey, Abby said you're here until the end of the month," he said. "What are you going to do while the rest of us are back in school on Tuesday?"

A zing raced through her when she realized he'd asked her cousin about her. "Going to school with you, I hope."

The feminine shriek and subsequent splash from behind her were music to Casey's ears.

"What do you mean you're going on a date?"

Missy bit back a smile at Liam's incredulous tone and

watched his gaze move from Casey to her and back again. The three of them sat at the huge center island in the Murphy kitchen, eating a late dinner of takeout pizza.

"Did you know about this?" he asked, looking at Missy again.

His surprised expression was so genuine, she almost felt sorry for him.

"Of course," she said. "Casey told me two days ago."

"She didn't tell me." Liam turned back to their daughter. "You didn't tell me."

Casey shrugged. "You've been busy."

"I told you," Missy said, stealing a piece of pepperoni from a half-eaten pie still in the box, "that same night."

"You did?" This came from Liam and Casey at the same time.

"Yes, I did." She lifted one shoulder in a casual shrug. "You replied with a mumbled 'that's nice' while your nose was stuck in a financial report. I figured you were—as Casey said—busy."

Too busy to care?

Missy hadn't wanted to think so, but a part of her had worried that Liam didn't think the news of Casey going out with a boy was a big deal. In his defense, he didn't have much experience at this, and the last two weeks had been hectic for all of them.

Her boss had pushed up the deadline for a design concept for a new film, a period piece set in the 1940s, due to start filming in the US next year, and Liam had had to deal with one work crisis after another, most of which kept him at his desk or on the phone long after the end of the workday.

Other than an overnight trip to Jackson Hole last weekend in which he'd flown the three of them in the company's helicopter—an amazing experience even if the trip had been business related for Liam—they hadn't seen much of each other.

Especially with Casey now attending Destiny High School.

She'd surprised them when she told them two days before school started that she'd changed her mind. Missy didn't have any idea how he'd arranged it—maybe with his brother's help after all—but Casey was now a full-time student with the understanding that she was expected to follow the same rules and guidelines as the other students, especially when it came to classwork.

Thanks to a review of her school records from London, she was allowed to take many of the same classes as Abby—something the young lady wasn't pleased about at all, at least according to Casey, who shared some of the snarky comments and subtle digs she'd been dealing with, both here and at school, all the while insisting her cousin's attitude wasn't a big deal and she didn't want anyone to know about how Abby was treating her.

Especially Liam.

"So where is this date taking place?" He dropped his uneaten piece of pizza to his plate and instead reached for his glass of wine. "And more importantly, with whom are you going?"

"The Star-Lite Drive-In and Nathan Lawson."

Liam choked on a mouthful of wine and both Casey and Missy slapped him on the back until he slipped off the stool and out of their reach.

"The d-drive-in?" he sputtered.

Casey nodded, confusion in her eyes. "Down near Laramie. Nathan says they close for the season at the end of the month and I've never been—are you okay?"

"Y-yeah." Liam pounded at his chest with a closed fist a few times, and then cleared his throat. "Yes, I'm fine."

"You look a wee bit pasty."

Missy had to agree with her daughter, but she wisely kept her mouth shut. Hmm, it seemed that the man did care that Casey had plans with a young lad for the evening.

That meant more to Missy than she'd thought it would.

"Sweetie, it's after seven," she said, noticing the time. "Didn't you say Nathan would be picking you up—"

"Bollocks! I've got to change my clothes, do my hair!" Chugging down the last of her milk, Casey raced for the door that led to the back deck and then stopped and spun back around. "Hey, we're not going to make a big production out of this, right?"

"If you mean do I want to meet him, then yes, we are," Missy said.

"Damn right we are." Liam's muttered words reached Missy, but thankfully they didn't seem to carry across the room.

"But that day in the pool—"

"He was just one of the crowd." Missy cut off her protest before it even began. "We were never introduced. You know the rules, Casey."

She sighed. "Fine, but please, let's keep this chill."

"In a house with this many people? We'll do our best."

Another eye roll, and Casey was gone. Missy turned around, glad to see that Liam had retaken his seat and regained his coloring. "Are you sure you're okay?"

He nodded. "I honestly didn't hear you the other night. Please, next time, make sure I respond to news like that with a comeback more intelligent. Like *not until she's thirty* or something."

That was sweet, but with just a couple of weeks left to their stay, Missy didn't think there would be a next time.

She ignored the pang in her chest and busied herself with cleaning up their mess. "Will do."

"Are you really okay with this?"

"I'll admit I was surprised when she first told me, but she has been out on group dates back home. She didn't mention it just now, but there are a bunch of kids going tonight. It's not like she's going to be alone with this Nathan." Missy put the box of leftover pizza in the refrigerator and tossed their used plates and napkins in the trash. "Besides, it seems the boy is a regular here at the house and he's a friend of Abby's. That's in his favor."

"The name sounds familiar."

"According to Casey he's the star quarterback of the football team and his father works for you."

Recognition shone in Liam's eyes. "Yes, Bill Lawson. One of our construction foremen. He's a good man."

"That's good to know."

"But Nathan is a senior. He might be eighteen already."

"He's not. His birthday isn't until next spring."

"And you know this how?"

Missy smiled. "Mothers and daughters do talk, you know. She's been bubbly about this boy since the group of them went out on the lake the Sunday before last."

"She's never mentioned him to me." Liam lifted a hand, cutting her off. "I know, I know. I've been busy."

"We all have been. The last two weeks have flown by."

As scared as Missy had been in coming here, even though she'd known it was the right thing—the only thing—to do, the last month had been wonderful...for Casey.

Liam and Casey seemed to be slowly finding their way with each other, especially since he'd found out Casey was keeping one of his guitars in her bedroom. And she'd surprised him in Jackson Hole when she sat at the baby grand piano located in their suite and gave a beautiful performance of a Mozart favorite.

But had they had enough time? Would the remaining days make their connection strong enough to survive being separated by so many miles? Being on two different continents?

How would she survive—

No! Missy blinked back the surprise sting of tears, refusing to allow her thoughts to even stray in that direction. She busied herself at the sink so as not to let Liam see her silly reaction.

This—none of this—was about her. Her and Liam.

There was no her and Liam.

He got to his feet and seconds later was at her side, leaning against the counter. "You know, spending twelve or fourteen hours buried in my work is the norm for me. Ever since I started working for the company full-time out of college. Especially after my dad semiretired and I moved into his job."

Thankful he hadn't picked up on her warring emotions, Missy could only nod, not trusting her voice yet.

"The last couple of weeks aside, I've gotten used to taking a lunch break every day, ending the workday in time for dinner."

Missy grabbed a towel and dried her hands. "Spoken like a man thinking with his stomach."

He leaned over and bumped her shoulder with his. "I was thinking about the people I've been sharing those meals with, and the times spent together afterward. I like having the two of you around."

And they liked being around him. More than they should.

"I think it's time we head outside to the deck so I can meet this young man," Missy said. "We wouldn't want Casey to sneak off on us."

"Would she do that?"

Missy grinned at him and, walking backward, headed for the door. "What were you doing when you were a teenager?"

Liam frowned, following her. "Yeah, that's what worries me."

The night air was warm as they stepped outside, even with the sun gone and twilight casting a glow over the yard. Casey was heading back toward them along the pathway, when a red pickup truck pulled into the lot.

"They're going in a truck. To the drive-in."

Missy looked at Liam, not surprised to find his arms crossed over his chest and a frown creasing his brow. "How did you think they were getting to the drive-in?" she asked. "On a bicycle?"

He remained silent, but at least he dropped his arms when the lad got out of the truck and headed toward them, nervously smoothing his hand down the front of his shirt as he approached the deck.

He smiled at Casey, but then turned to Missy and said, "Hi, you must be Casey's mother. I'm Nathan Lawson."

She took his outstretched hand, impressed that he'd spoken first. "Hi, Nathan. It's nice to meet you. I'm guessing you already know Casey's—"

The widening of her daughter's eyes conveyed an unspoken panic.

"Uh, Liam Murphy." Missy quickly amended the introduction, surprised that she'd been about to introduce him as Casey's father.

Casey had yet to call him that in front of her—in front of anyone—so Missy made the effort not to do so as well.

"Yes, ma'am, my father has worked for the Murphys for years." Nathan released her, and then held out his hand toward Liam. "It's good to see you again, sir."

Liam's shoulders relaxed a bit as he took the boy's hand. "You, too. What are your plans for the night?"

Casey sputtered, but Nathan shot her a quick smile and said, "We're meeting some friends at Sherry's Diner in town and then caravanning to the drive-in. There's about ten of us going in three cars."

"What time do you plan to have her home?"

"Crikey!" Casey managed to find her voice, and it was edgy. "It's a double feature! We'll be back after the movie ends."

"Well, actually, Coach has the entire team on a curfew, so we'll have to leave before the end of the second movie. She'll be home by midnight." Nathan looked at his date again. "Hope that's okay with you."

Casey's blustering vanished and she smiled shyly. "That's fine." She then turned imploring eyes to Missy. "We should go. Like Nathan said, there are others waiting for us."

Missy glanced at Liam, who seemed ready to say something else, but she placed a hand on his arm and turned back to her daughter. "Have fun."

The two kids nodded and headed for Nathan's truck. Missy couldn't hear what her daughter was saying—probably apologizing for putting him through that—but the lad only laughed. He walked Casey to the passenger side, held the door for her as she climbed in and then jogged around the front and got in behind the wheel. Nice touch.

"I wasn't done with him yet."

"I'm sure. What were you going to do next?" She could feel his muscles clenching beneath her fingers and she dropped her hand away. "Ask to see the lad's driver's license?"

When Liam remained silent, Missy turned to face him, but he was watching the pickup as it left the parking lot.

She could see the worry on his face and found his concern for their daughter endearing.

"She's going to be fine."

"She's in a truck. With a teenage boy."

"So?"

"So I—we—that used to be me. Used to be us." Liam looked at her, his expression different now, his eyes taking on a darker emotion. "Please tell me you remember what we were doing in my pickup when we were seventeen."

A heated flush stole over her cheeks. Of course she remembered. "That was different."

"How so?"

"For one, Casey isn't seventeen, and this is a first date." Missy fought against the flood of memories filling her head. Her heart. "You and I had been together for a while before things got…involved."

"A couple of months." Liam reached for her then, putting one hand at her waist and cupping her cheek with the other as he stepped closer. "If memory serves, we couldn't seem to keep our hands off each other."

"Hey, don't mind us," came a male voice, the words laced with laughter.

Missy sprang back from Liam's touch, surprised to find Adam and Fay heading toward them, smiles on their faces. "Oh! Hello…we didn't know you two were here."

"Yeah, we can see that."

Fay swatted at her husband. "We just dropped off A.J. and we saw you two out here and wondered if you have plans for the evening."

"I think we're going to the drive-in," Liam said.

"We are not," Missy countered, knowing Casey would be horrified to find them spying on her. "We most certainly are not."

Adam threw them a questioning look before saying,

"Okay, then come with us. Bobby and Leeann Winslow are officially closing the camp tonight with a bonfire." He glanced at Missy. "Leeann said we should invite the two of you. Do you remember her? She was Leeann Harris back then. She graduated with you and Liam."

"Yes, of course, I remember her."

Missy had run into a few former classmates over the last weeks: Racy Dillon, now married to the local sheriff, who owned the Blue Creek Saloon, and Maggie—whose last name Missy couldn't remember. Maggie had happily introduced the handsome cowboy with her as her husband, Landon Cartwright.

As for tonight, Missy had planned to get some work done while waiting up for Casey, but now she thought a distraction for Liam, one that involved other people, was probably a good idea.

"I think a bonfire sounds like jolly fun," she said with a smile. "I haven't been to one since…well, since I was a teenager."

"Well, I guess that's settled." Liam stepped in close again, one hand to the small of her back, his words a low whisper in her ear. "I, for one, am all for reliving *our* youthful past. Each and every moment of it."

Chapter Ten

"Are you having fun?" Liam asked.

Missy peeked at him over the rim of her red plastic cup, the glow from the roaring campfire highlighting the mischievous sparkle in her eyes.

"I've asked you that before."

She lowered the cup, a soft smile on her beautiful lips. "A few times, and the answer is still the same. Yes, I'm having fun."

Liam returned her grin, feeling foolish and happy at the same time. Unbelievably happy. Despite the nagging irritation over Casey being out with that boy tonight, he was finally alone on a date himself, with Missy.

Well, as alone as one could be in this crowd.

He looked around at the group sitting around the outdoor fire pit at Camp Diamond, the kids' camp his friends Bobby and Leeann Winslow had opened this summer. Liam and his family had been contracted to construct all of the buildings, and from what he'd heard tonight, the camp's inaugural season had been a big success.

With the sun long gone, there was a hint of fall crispness in the air as the dark sky put on a show with an abundance of stars and a full moon shining overhead. Except for the office, the rest of the camp buildings were dark, allowing the fire to create a warm beacon that gave off just enough light to see the water lapping at the edge of the lake a few feet away.

There'd been quite a crowd here already when Liam, Missy, Adam and Fay showed up. Maggie and Racy, Leeann's close friends, sat in folding chairs next to Missy, along with their husbands, while Gina and Justin Dillon were beside him.

Family and friends, gathered together. Just as it should be. And somehow it felt right having Missy here with him.

Bobby and Leeann had seats on the opposite side of the fire pit with Dean Zippenella and Priscilla Lennox next to them, but at the moment Bobby's best friend, Dean, was chasing after a couple of four-legged guests. The camp's official mascots were dogs that belonged to Dean and Priscilla, who'd come to town this past summer to help with fund-raising for the camp. Last month's bachelor auction had been Priscilla's idea.

The funds raised that night hadn't been substantial, less than five thousand dollars, and a good chunk of that had been from Priscilla bidding two grand to win a date with Dean. She'd been competing with her own sister, no less. The important thing was the event had brought the town together to support the camp—and had brought Dean and Priscilla together, too, as they were now living in Dean's log home along with their pups.

In fact, Liam noticed all the couples here tonight were married, except for Dean and Priscilla.

And him and Missy.

Leaning forward, he propped his elbows on his knees and poked at the fire with a long stick, sending a shower of fiery sparks into the air. He looked at Missy, enjoying the view of her profile and how her hair and skin glowed in the firelight as she talked with Maggie and Landon. He wondered if she too had noticed how everyone sat boy-girl-boy-girl around the fire. It hadn't started out that way.

When they'd first arrived, Leeann had taken her on a quick tour of the camp, most of the ladies tagging along while the men argued good-naturally over the best way to get the fire going. But once everyone gathered at the fire pit, they naturally paired off and Missy had come to sit beside him, accepting the cup of wine he'd poured for her and the old plaid blanket he draped across both their laps to ward off the night's chill.

"Hey, how about some music?" Racy asked. "I bullied Gage into bringing his guitar, as he only seems to serenade our babies nowadays."

"That's not true," Gage protested with a wide grin, reaching for the instrument stowed beneath his chair. "I sang you an Elvis tune in the shower just this morning."

"Which I had to listen to over the baby monitor while changing a pair of stinky diapers. So romantic!"

Everyone laughed as Dean and Priscilla came back to join them, along with their worn-out pups, a wiry terrier mutt and a Chihuahua wearing a bright red sweater, both of whom curled up beneath their chairs.

Liam set aside the stick to grab his own guitar, glad he'd thought to bring it along as well. But doing so had his thoughts turning to Casey.

Maybe getting her enrolled at the local high school hadn't been his best idea. He'd wanted her to have fun during her stay and get to know some people her own age, and yeah, he'd hoped for some alone time with Missy.

That hadn't worked out so well due to one work crisis after another, until tonight, but even that was only because Casey was out on a date.

With a boy.

Correction, with a group, much like the crowd here, but had those kids paired off as easily as the adults? What exactly was going on at the drive-in?

If personal experience served, he knew exactly what was going on.

Damn. He rubbed at his chest.

The heaviness that had settled there as he'd watched that boy's pickup truck drive off now seemed to have doubled in weight. It wasn't painful, but definitely unfamiliar.

He wasn't used to...well, worrying about someone.

He had a normal concern for his folks, especially when they took off on one of their cross-country adventures in their tricked-out RV, and caring about his brothers and their families was as natural to him as breathing, but this wasn't the same.

Not nearly the same.

"I'm glad you brought your guitar, too." Missy gave his knee a nudge with her own beneath the blanket. "It'd be nice to hear you sing again."

Liam grinned, her words pulling him from his thoughts. "I'm afraid I'm not much better than I was years ago. Which we both know wasn't that good."

"You were great with Casey."

"That was all her. I just tried to keep up."

"Your daughter plays?" Racy asked, and when Missy nodded, she continued, "I guess she gets that from Liam, huh?"

"Yes, she does," Missy said. "My creativity begins and

ends with my design work, I fear. I have zero talent when it comes to music."

Liam managed to keep his gaze on Gage, joining in when the man started strumming a classic Johnny Cash tune, but inside he was bursting with pride at Missy's words.

Not just over the connection she'd made between him and Casey, but the ease with which she'd spoken about their daughter. He'd figured there'd be questions. Missy had told him the ladies had asked about Casey when they first arrived. Nothing invasive, just a natural curiosity over an unusual situation, especially for a town the size of Destiny.

They'd somehow managed to keep the whole truth from everyone, including his family. Things were going well and the last thing he wanted was any upheaval when he was making so much headway with Casey and Missy.

The sound of applause yanked Liam from his thoughts and he found the first song was over. The sheriff gave him a quick nod that meant it was his turn to pick the next one. He went with another classic, this time one from the Fab Four, earning a big smile from Missy, who joined in as they sang about welcoming the sun after a long winter. After that they went through a half dozen tunes until he and Gage begged off, insisting they needed some liquid refreshment.

"I was wondering something," Missy said to Liam after he refilled her cup. "How did the camp get its name?"

"Ask those two." Liam pointed across the fire as he called out to Bobby, "Hey, Missy wants to know about Camp Diamond's name."

"It's all Leeann's fault," Bobby said.

"It is not!" Leeann protested. "Who told you to toss it in the lake?"

Bobby barked out a quick laugh and then turned sober.

"Okay, that was all me. It's amazing to hear us joke about it now. You see, I'd asked Leeann to marry me during our senior year."

"Really?" Missy looked surprised. "I don't remember that."

"We tried to keep it a secret. Our parents weren't happy about us being together back then," Leeann said. "But just before graduation I panicked and broke things off. I gave the ring back—"

Bobby cut her off. "More like chucked it at my head. But she's right, I was the one who heaved the ring into the lake on my way out of town. It wasn't much, barely a chip, but after that, I always called this place Diamond Lake."

"And the ring is still down there?"

Leeann nodded. "As far as we know. After Bobby told me what he'd done all those years ago, I gave him the lake, and the land around it, for the camp. Before I even knew if he'd decided to go ahead with building it."

"What a wonderful story."

"Yeah, just not one we share around the fire with the campers," Bobby added, with a grin. "No need to give them any ideas."

"Well, you've done good here, Winslow," Liam said to his friend. "This camp was just what the town needed."

Everyone joined in while Bobby tried to wave off the praise. Then he placed a hand over Leeann's rounded belly and cradled her on his lap. "If it wasn't for the love of my life coming back *into* my life, none of this would have happened."

"Let's hear it for the ladies," Justin Dillon said, coming up behind Gina, wrapping one arm around his wife's waist while raising his beer in the air with the other. "If it wasn't for them, we'd all be lost and lonely bums."

Everyone joined in on the toast and then Gina said,

"Looks like the town is going to have one less bum running around. Or one less bachelor."

Liam wasn't sure what she meant, until Landon pointed toward the water's edge in time for everyone to watch Dean drop to one knee before what appeared to be a very surprised Priscilla.

Moments later, she was in his arms with Dean shouting at them, "She said yes!"

There were more cheers, congratulatory hugs and handshakes when the couple returned to the fire and Priscilla showed off a large diamond solitaire on her finger. Liam placed a quick kiss on her cheek and then shook Dean's hand, offering his best wishes.

"I thought they'd only just met."

Missy's words were quiet, meant only for his ears as Liam returned to the bench and sat next to her.

"Priscilla came to town just after July Fourth, so yeah, it's only been a couple of months." He turned to her, threading his fingers through hers, noticing how warm, how right, it felt to hold her hand. "When it's the right person, why wait?"

The party broke up an hour later. Liam glanced at the clock on the dashboard as he drove back to the ranch. It was almost eleven thirty. Missy hadn't said anything, but he guessed she wanted to be home before Casey got back from her date.

Hell, he wanted to be there as well to make sure their daughter arrived home safely.

On the other hand, he hated to see this night end.

Being with Missy tonight was like old times. Familiar, comfortable. But at the same time a thread of a new awareness, a new excitement, coursed through him every time he looked at her. Touched her. When she'd rested her head against his shoulder and looked up at him with a riot of emotions reflected in her eyes, he'd almost said the words aloud.

She was the first girl he'd fallen in love with. She was a woman he desperately wanted now in his bed. In his home. In his life in every way possible.

She was breaking his heart all over again.

Not really, not yet, but tonight made him realize his time with her and Casey was quickly coming to an end. Or was it? He had to admit the crazy idea of the two of them making the move to Destiny a permanent one had been gaining traction for the last week.

He just wasn't sure how to make the suggestion, how Missy would react or if she was even battling the same needs and wants as he was.

"You made a comment back at the fire tonight that has me wondering about something."

Missy's quiet words filled the silence of the SUV, and he immediately started to mentally backtrack.

They'd talked about a lot of things. Memories from high school. How the town had changed over the years. The bachelor auction. Liam had made it clear his date had ended with nothing more than a simple kiss—

"When you said time didn't matter. Is that what you felt before?"

Okay, he was totally lost. "Before?"

"When you proposed? I guess you believed those women were right for you…at the time."

Her question floored him. They hadn't talked about his previous marriages at all after the first night she'd arrived. And it wasn't exactly a topic he wanted to bring up now, but since she'd asked, he said, "I honestly don't remember. The first time was a crazy, stupid, alcohol-laced quickie in Vegas. I figured out not long afterward how unfair our marriage was...to her and to me."

"Unfair?"

He glanced at her. "I was trying to get over losing you. And failing miserably."

She gasped softly and the glow from the dashboard allowed him to see her press her fingers to her lips.

He focused again on the road as he turned onto the lane that led to the compound. "When I decided to marry for the second time," he continued, "it was right out of college. Nicole and I had dated for a couple of years, so marriage seemed like the next step after we graduated."

"What happened?"

"After a year we finally admitted we wanted different things." Pulling into his usual parking spot, he turned off the engine and cut the lights, his hands gripping hard at the steering wheel. "She hated the fact that I chose to stay in Destiny and work for the family business. She wanted bigger and better things. So she left to find them."

Making him a loser twice over. Three times, actually, counting Missy.

He dropped his hands, curling his keys into his fist as silence again stretched between them. For such an intimate setting, it felt as if she was now farther away from him than just the next seat.

Almost as if there was an ocean between them.

"And you never found the right person after that?"

The dull ache in the center of his chest returned, but he refused to acknowledge it, no matter how desperately he wanted to rub the pain away.

"Nope. There was no need." He opened his door. "I'd already found the right girl, but I wasn't smart enough to hold onto her."

He got out of the truck before she had the chance to say anything.

By the time he made it around the back end to Missy's door, she was already standing outside. She remained silent as they started walking along the pathway through the yard, passing by the gazebo.

"It's still so bright out here," she said. "Shouldn't most of the accent lighting be off by this time?"

After what he'd said to her back at the truck, this was what she wanted to talk about?

Liam sighed. Not that he was interested in talking anymore tonight. No, what he wanted to do was grab her, pull her into his arms and find other uses for that pretty mouth of hers. Find out if his feelings were all one-sided, or if she was trying to sort through some crazy emotions as well.

He shoved his hands in his pockets to keep from doing what he desired. "I overrode the shutdown remotely from my phone while we were out."

"Why…oh." She looked at him, her lips pursed as if she was attempting to hold back a smile. Or blow him a kiss. "You didn't want Casey to be alone in the dark with her date."

"Damn right I didn't."

Her soft laughter rippled over his skin like caressing fingers. "You know, she might be home already."

Liam looked up as they approached the boathouse; the apartment was still dark except for a small glow from the living area. "Are you kidding? If she's anything like we were, she'll push the curfew right up to the last minute."

"Well, since there's plenty of light out here, you don't have to see me back to the flat."

They stepped onto the path that led along the side of the boathouse, the shadows darker and deeper here. "A gentleman always sees his date to her door."

"And you're a gentleman?"

"I'm trying my best."

She stopped, her touch warm on his already heated skin. "What if I don't want you to be?"

Hoping he was reading her words correctly, he gave in to the need raging in him. He stopped too and reached for her, one hand landing on the small of her back, anchoring her against him. He cupped her head with his other hand, his fingers digging into the soft strands of her hair, holding her in place as his mouth came down on hers.

A spike of heat started low in his gut. A moan escaped Missy's lips as she parted to accept his kiss.

She grabbed at his arms, not to push him away but to hold on as they stumbled backward together, deeper into the darkness, into the corner, until the rough texture of the log wall scratched the backs of his hands.

Longing that had been building since the last time they kissed twisted in his gut. She had to feel the same, with the way she met the forceful demand of his kisses with demands of her own. He moved his hand down past her hips to cup her perfect backside. But only for a moment—then he slid them up again along the softness of her shirt until he found her breast, his thumb automatically scraping lightly across the hardened tip—

She stiffened and broke free from his mouth. "Liam, wait."

He lifted both his hands from her and moved to take a step away, but she stopped him. "No, I don't—I thought I heard—oh, my, headlights."

Liam looked over his shoulder in time to see the harsh glare, but then it was gone. Seconds later the sound of a vehicle engine being shut down and doors opening and then closing filled the air.

"It's Casey," Missy's words came out in a whisper. "She's home!"

And she wasn't alone. Liam could hear his daughter's sweet laughter, and unintelligible words in a lower, masculine tone. They were headed this way, cutting through the yard on the far side of Nolan's place, taking the most direct route to the boathouse.

Meaning they would be here any minute.

He grabbed Missy's hand. "Come on."

"What—"

Yanking open a nearby door, he stepped inside the small space, pulling her behind him. "In here."

"Where are we?" she whispered.

"The outdoor shower." The door gently bumped closed behind them and Liam receded as far as he could, until he felt the cold metal pipes and fixtures pressed against his back. Missy followed, her backside against his front. He tightened his hands on her waist, biting back a groan at how perfectly she fit there.

"Liam, we shouldn't…" She leaned her head back into his chest, her words still a low whisper.

"Shh, they're right outside." He dipped his head, his mouth at her ear.

Moments later, they clearly heard two sets of footsteps as Casey and Nathan walked past them.

"You know, you don't have to walk me all the way to the flat," Casey said, sounding just like her mother a few minutes ago.

"Sure I do," Nathan replied. "My dad taught me I should always make sure my date gets safely home."

Missy looked over her shoulder at him and smiled.

Yeah, okay. The kid got points for that.

"That's sweet, but I'm sure my mum is waiting up for

me. I can go from here. The last thing you'd want is to be..." Casey's voice faded as they continued walking.

Although Liam could hear a deep chuckle that had to be Nathan's, they were too far away now for him to hear what they were saying. Setting Missy aside, he stepped toward the door, easing it open a crack. Just enough to—

"What are you doing?" She hissed in his ear. "Spying on them?"

"Yes."

She rolled her eyes, but then moved in front of him again, crouching a bit so both of them could look at what was happening out there.

Liam spotted his daughter and her date standing in a pool of light at the far end of the boathouse. It was a familiar scene, as if he was seeing himself and Missy, just like that, years ago. Needing to say good-night, but not wanting the night to end. Neither of them sure of what the next move should be.

Nathan stood with his thumbs tucked into his back pockets, Casey rocking up on her toes a bit. Their voices were too soft to hear. Then, all at once, Casey placed her hands lightly on her date's shoulders and reached up, giving him a kiss on the lips that lasted far longer than Liam liked before she spun away, her footsteps echoing on the stairs that led up to the apartment.

The boy remained rooted to the spot for a moment. Then he shook his head and headed back toward them. Liam wasn't sure he liked the goofy grin on Nathan's face, but he allowed the door to shut again when the kid got close, staying perfectly still until he heard the sound of the boy's truck starting up and leaving the parking lot.

"That was sweet," Missy said.

That was close.

Their daughter had almost found her parents making out

right outside the boathouse. Then again, if he and Missy had made it up to the apartment, she might've walked in on them necking on the sofa like a couple of teen—

Liam slammed a lid on that thought, raking his fingers through his hair.

"Hey, are you all right?"

No, he was far from all right.

Liam looked down at her, surprised that his emotions had switched so fast from worrying about their daughter to wanting nothing more than to pick up where he and Missy had left off.

He wanted her in his arms, wanted his mouth, his hands, on her. Wanted her hands on him.

Missy must've been able to read the desire in his eyes, because she turned, pushed the shower door open and stepped back into the cool night air. He followed, taking her arm to stop her when she started to walk away.

She stilled, pulling from his touch, but she did turn back to face him. "I should go. Casey is probably waiting for me."

"And worrying?"

Missy shook her head. "I left her a note."

That surprised him. "Telling her you were out with me?"

"Telling her that you and I went to see some old friends and I would be back around the same time as she."

And she would've been if he hadn't given in to the crazy need to have this woman in his arms again. But it wasn't just him. Missy had been willing, too; she wanted that kiss as much as he did.

Why was she now acting as if nothing had happened between them?

"I want you."

She slowly lifted her gaze to his, the astonishment in her eyes cutting him.

"Please don't tell me that surprises you."

"We can't…we can't let the past—*our* past—affect our lives now."

"Why not?" he demanded.

She took a step back, pulled in a quick breath and squared her shoulders, her posture perfectly ballerina straight now. "I've already told you, I'm here because of Casey, to give her a chance to get to know you and your family."

"Do you really believe that? You were the one who put out an obvious invite a few minutes ago. Now you're giving me mixed signals."

"I'm sorry. I shouldn't—we shouldn't have—"

"Oh, yeah, we should." He stepped closer. "Are you going to hide behind Casey and deny you still have feelings for me?"

"Of course I have feelings for you. How could I not?" Missy's response came in a cool, distant tone, despite how much her admission surprised him. "But this trip isn't about me, about us. It never was. The last thing I'm going to do is to let myself think, to dream… I did that once and I got my heart crushed. I won't do it again. Not even for you."

"Missy, I would never—"

"Please…don't." She moved back again, holding out a hand this time to ward him off from following her. "Please don't make a promise we both know you can't—that neither of us can keep."

Chapter Eleven

Liam stared at the envelope in his hand, his heart beating so loudly in his chest he was certain it could be heard even here on the sidewalk outside Destiny's medical clinic on a busy Friday afternoon.

"I was about to head out to your place when I saw you drive by." Dr. Ronald Cody, the only full-time physician they had in Destiny, looked more like a cowboy in his worn leather boots and white Stetson instead of a stethoscope and a white jacket.

Dr. Cody had just flagged Liam down as he drove along East Main Street. When Liam had first seen the doctor waving at him, he'd feared the worst. That something had happened to someone in the family—to Missy or Casey—while he'd been on a return flight from a two-day business trip in Denver.

He'd hated leaving on Wednesday, but he hadn't been able to reschedule the meeting. The crazy idea of asking

Missy to come with him had crossed his mind during one of his many sleepless nights since their date, but he knew she'd never agree to go.

Hell, they'd barely spoken to each other in the last week.

Short of coming right out and demanding time with her, he couldn't get her alone so they could continue their unfinished conversation about the two of them.

At least it was unfinished on his end.

Missy had that British stiff-upper-lip thing so down pat no one else seemed to notice how she was being aloof, even when it was just him, her and Casey.

Not that there'd been many of those times recently.

His fingers tightened around the envelope, remembering the fleeting glimpses of confusion he'd seen in Missy's eyes over the last few days when she thought no one was looking.

And he'd put them there. His fault. He hated that and they needed to talk—

"Liam?" The doctor's voice cut off the memory. "You okay?"

"Yes, I'm fine, and thank you." Forcing a smile, Liam relaxed his grip and held out his other hand. "For getting this back to me."

"I'm sorry it took so long, but a computer glitch caused quite a backup at the lab." The doctor returned his handshake. "I'm sure you want to open that somewhere more private. It's pretty self-explanatory, but if you need to talk, just call the office."

Somewhere more private.

An image popped into Liam's head, so clear it was like looking at a photograph. Him, Missy and Casey. Yeah, as much as he wanted to get Missy alone, he wanted even more to share this moment with their daughter, too.

Especially because of what he planned on *not* doing.

Heading back to his truck, he checked his watch. There was still time to make a few stops. The grocery store, the butcher shop. And he'd swing into Fay's to grab a bouquet of flowers before heading home.

But he was going to need some help, and he knew exactly whom to ask.

He pulled out his cell phone as he slipped behind the wheel. "Hey, Mom," he said after the call went through. "Yeah, I'm back in town, but keep that to yourself, okay? And I need a favor."

Less than an hour later, he arrived at the house, surprised at finding a group of all-terrain vehicles sitting in the parking lot, one with a trailer attached to the back.

After exiting his vehicle, he grabbed his bags from the backseat as Nolan came around the side of his house, the twins with him, their arms loaded with boxes, a couple of axes and sleeping bags.

"You're back. How did the meeting go?" Nolan asked.

"As expected. The deal is closed." Liam joined his brother and nephews at the three-wheelers. "What's going on here?"

"The boys and I are going to winterize the north cabin this weekend." Nolan secured a crate he'd been carrying in the trailer. "Lay in supplies, chop a few cords of wood, the usual."

Liam nodded. He'd forgotten that was this weekend. The cabin was used year-round, as it was situated right in the center of their woodland acreage. With only one bedroom, it was small, but bunk racks in the main living space allowed for up to six people to stay there as long as they didn't mind roughing it. Other than a small generator, the place was pretty much off the grid when it came to modern amenities.

Because of the cabin's remote location, ATVs and horseback were the only ways to get there. In the past, at least two of the Murphy brothers had gone, Devlin usually being one. Of course, he was in England now. Getting Bryant away from his pregnant wife was probably going to be a tough sell. That left Liam or Adam.

"Hey, you aren't looking for company, are you?" Liam asked.

Nolan grinned. "Why? You want to get out of that suit and rough it for the next couple of days?"

Not really. "Ah—"

"Don't worry, I think I've got all the company I need," his brother said, slanting his head in the direction of the twins. "It's about time these Muggles earned their keep."

"Well, have a good time."

Liam started for his place, thinking he should get the steaks he bought into the refrigerator when the sight of Casey and Missy heading his way stopped him. They were talking and neither saw him standing there, but the same duffel bag Casey had had with her the day they met was slung over one shoulder.

"Oh, hey, you're back." The smile that lit up Casey's face when she spotted him pierced straight through the envelope tucked away in his inside jacket pocket and smacked him right in the heart. "I was hoping I'd see you before I left."

He glanced over his shoulder at the ATVs again, counting the vehicles parked there. Yeah, her plans weren't hard to figure out, and there went his.

"Left?" he asked anyway, hoping he might be wrong.

"Just for the weekend." This came from Abby, who skipped down the steps from her house, a similar bag over her shoulder and another in her arms. "We're still lucky enough to have her company for another ten days. What fun!"

Liam caught his niece's bright smile from the corner of his eye as she walked past, but his gaze was on Casey, who turned her back to her cousin and rolled her eyes. "Did I mention she's started a countdown?"

"Are you sure you want to go?" Missy asked.

"Of course. I'm not going to let some nippy—" Casey glanced his way and snapped her mouth closed for a moment before she sighed. "I never should've told her that you got our tickets. She caught me in a moment of weakness after tipping me off about Nat—the jerk who shall be nameless. Besides, I want to drive that ATV again."

"With a helmet," Missy added.

Again with the eye roll. "Of course."

"Wait a minute," Liam said, feeling the need to catch up as Casey switched from topic to topic. "What is Abby counting down to, what tickets are you talking about and why is Nathan now a jerk? Did he try anything with you—"

"Ah, look at the flowers. Yellow roses, nice." Casey cut him off, placing a hand on his arm as she pushed up on her toes and peeked into the top of the grocery bag he carried. "Crikey, you got a bunch there. Planning something special?"

Liam tried hard to keep up with his daughter. "Actually, I was hoping to cook dinner for you and your mother tonight."

"That's sweet. I didn't know you cooked."

"I can manage a barbecue grill as well as the next guy."

Casey's gaze flew from him to her mother and then to where Nolan and his kids were milling around the three-wheelers. "Well, I guess I could cancel my plans…"

Her voice trailed off, but he could see how much she wanted to go to the cabin. It meant a lot to him that she'd offered to stick around. They'd had a great time last weekend when he taught her how to ride the all-terrain vehicles his family kept at the compound. He didn't want to be responsible for her missing the chance to ride again.

The test results could wait. He'd already accepted the truth.

"No, don't do that." Liam said. "We can do this another night."

"You sure?" Casey asked.

"Very sure." He grabbed one of the bundles of roses from the bag and presented it to her. "Here, something to decorate the cabin."

"Cool!"

"And please, do what your mother said. Wear all of your protective gear while driving and listen to—"

"Yeah, I know. Do everything Uncle Nolan says, stay on the trails and no going over the designated speed limit." Casey buried her nose in the flowers for a moment, and then gave him another big smile. "You know, you should still cook for my mum. She got some great news today!"

Liam enjoyed the pink blush on Missy's cheeks. Maybe his plans for the evening weren't a total bust after all. "Really? What's that?"

"Oh, it's nothing." Missy shook her head. "Just something related to my clothing line."

"Hey, finding out Princess Kate purchased one of your formal frocks isn't nothing," Casey said, caressing one of the rosebuds. "Can you imagine what's going to happen when the future queen shows up at some high-society fling in a Melissa Ellington original? Your sales are going to go through the roof!"

"I agree with Casey. That sounds like a pretty big deal." Liam grinned at Missy, happy when she returned his smile. "And a perfect reason for us to celebrate."

She almost hadn't come.

Foolish as that seemed now, walking along the pathway

from the boathouse to his place in the soft, diffused twilight, Missy had been tempted to call Liam and tell him getting together was not a good idea.

Especially after his mother had made a big deal about her, Alistair, Bryant and Laurie going out tonight for dinner and a show in Cheyenne. With Nolan and the kids gone, that meant she and Liam were the only ones in the compound.

A fact that made it clear why canceling their plans would have been the right thing to do. For her. For him. For everyone.

But she couldn't do it.

Tired of debating with herself when deep inside she'd already accepted the fact she wanted to be with him tonight, she'd taken a quick shower and then slipped into a simple top, a long, flowing skirt that reached her ankles and a pair of flats. She'd studied her reflection in the mirror after applying her makeup, and thought about leaving her hair loose, but ended up putting it in the familiar chignon style she normally wore.

Yes, normal was what she was going for.

Tonight was just another normal night. Dinner with a man who just happened to be the father of her child…and the only man she'd ever loved.

Past tense, of course.

"Oh, you're a bloody liar," she whispered, her words floating on the cool night air. "Why can't you just admit what you want?"

Lifting the hem of her skirt to keep from tripping, she took the stairs to Liam's front porch. A quick intake of breath and she knocked before she could think about it.

Nothing. She knocked again and thought she heard him call out her name. She opened the door and peeked inside. "Liam?"

"Yeah, come on in. I'm—" A loud clanging filled the air. "Damn! I'm back in the kitchen."

Stepping inside the front foyer, Missy closed the door behind her, the sight of bright yellow roses in a vase on the entry table making her smile.

She'd only been inside Liam's home once before, when he'd given her and Casey a tour one afternoon, but she remembered the kitchen ran along the back of the log house. There was a wide timber stairway directly in front of her that led to the second floor, and his office and an empty guest room were on the right. She turned left and walked into the living room.

A fire was already lit in the fireplace, reflecting off the leather furniture arranged in front of the stone hearth. She headed for the dining area that opened into the oversize kitchen, noticing the large table was beautifully set at one end with matching place mats, cloth napkins, sparkling dishes, tapered candles, an open bottle of wine and more of those beautiful roses.

And the distinct odor of something...burning?

"Liam? Is everything okay?"

He slammed the lids on a couple of stainless steel pots and spun around from the stove, looking adorable with a dishcloth tucked into the waistband of his jeans as a make-shift apron. "Define okay?"

She moved to the counter that separated the two spaces, noticing how his dark hair stood in spiky tufts, as if he'd run his hands through it a few times. His white T-shirt hugged his muscular chest nicely, highlighting the dark shadow of his tattoo and the splattering of multicolored food stains across the front.

"Is that our dinner I smell?" she asked.

"If it smells like burned rubber, then, yeah, I guess it is."

"It's not that bad," she said, noticing that the two sets

of French doors that led out to the rear deck were open, along with the windows over the sink, allowing the night air to clear out the kitchen. "Can I do anything to help?"

"Yeah, pour us a glass of wine. I need it." He grabbed a wooden spoon and turned back to the stove.

Missy tried to hide her smile as she did what he asked, but the furrow of his brow made it hard to resist as she joined him again, two glasses of wine in her hands. "Here."

He reached for one, and then paused and wiped his hands across the towel at his front before taking it from her. "Thanks, I really need this."

"I can see that." She started to check one of the pots, but his fingers, warm and firm, landed on hers before she could lift the lid. "What's in here?"

He took a large gulp. "Burned rice."

She slid from his touch and this time only pointed at a second pot. "And that?"

"Broccoli." His tone was unforgiving. "Also burned."

She didn't ask about the third pan. A quick sniff spoke of extra-crispy carrots, and not in a good way. "Please tell me you haven't gotten the steaks on the grill yet."

His sharp gaze swung to her, but then a moment later humor replaced the hardness in his cool blue eyes and he grinned. "No, not yet."

"Well, thank goodness for that."

Liam sighed and looked again at the mess on the stove. "I don't know what happened. I came home, put the groceries away, grabbed a quick shower and then started getting things ready."

The smoothness of his jaw told her he'd shaved again as well. The familiar scent of his woodsy cologne made it through the lingering kitchen odors to tickle her nose and dredge up old memories.

Taking a step back, she sipped from her wine. "So, what happened? Trying to do too many dishes at once?"

"No, I think I was distracted."

Missy looked around the kitchen. "By what?"

"The thought of you and me. Alone. In my house."

His words brought her gaze back to his, and the intensity of his look made her fingers tighten around her glass.

"I kept waiting for my phone to ring," he finally said. "For you to back out on dinner."

She closed her eyes, nibbling on her bottom lip to stop herself from confirming his suspicions.

"I'm really glad you didn't."

His words were soft, but she could hear them clearly, feel the warmth of them on her face, telling her he'd closed the distance between them.

She opened her eyes to find him right in front of her. "I'm glad I didn't, too."

He grinned and she noticed a smudge of something—mashed carrots, maybe—on one cheek. "So, I guess I should get back to figuring out what we're going to eat tonight."

She had a better idea. "How about we get a little teamwork going?"

"What do you mean?"

"Do you have the makings for a salad? Maybe a couple of potatoes?"

He nodded. "In the fridge."

"Why don't you get cleaned up?" Unable to resist, she brushed the small orange blotch from his face with the tip of her finger. "And then you can concentrate on the steaks. I'll see what I can do about side dishes."

He grabbed her hand, brought it to his mouth and placed a kiss at her wrist. "Don't touch anything. I clean up my own messes."

Her breath caught, rendering her speechless. All she could do was nod and tug her hand free, oddly disappointed when he let her go.

"I'll be right back."

"I'll be here."

An hour later they sat at the dining room table, lingering over what had turned out to be a great meal. Liam was now wearing a pale blue button-down shirt hanging loose over his hips with the sleeves rolled back, but was still in jeans and barefoot.

He'd proved to be as skilled at manning a barbecue as he'd claimed; the steaks were perfect. The simple garden salad and grilled potatoes she'd whipped up while he'd filled the dishwasher with the remnants of his culinary disasters had been good complements, if she did say so herself.

Their conversation while they ate had been easy. She'd shown him the text from Casey letting her know they'd arrived at the cabin. He'd told her about getting a call from Nolan and then shared funny stories about trips to the cabin over the years with his brothers and friends.

He'd then told her about his successful meeting in Denver with a well-known political figure they were going to build a home for. She had in turn confessed her joy over a member of the royal family buying one of her designs and what it might mean to her business.

Now as they sat here after dinner, he asked about the tickets Casey had mentioned earlier, a shadow passing over his eyes when Missy told him that their return flight to London was all set for a week from Monday.

Then the subject turned to Casey and Nathan. Missy relayed why their daughter now considered the lad a jerk—

apparently she'd caught him kissing someone else, a former girlfriend who'd moved back to Destiny just this week.

"And it was Abby who warned Casey to this kid's two-timing?" Liam asked.

Missy nodded. "Apparently she pointed out the two mid-kiss to Casey during the school day, which does surprise me, as the two of them haven't actually gotten along too well during our stay."

"Yeah, I noticed her attitude a few times, but then again, Abby's always been...opinionated."

Spoiled was more like it, but Missy kept silent about that assessment. Casey had made it clear from the beginning she'd wanted to find her own way when it came to her cousin.

And now they only had ten days left in their visit.

Then what? Surely Liam would want to continue the relationship he'd forged with their daughter. Would he expect Casey to fly to Destiny for her school breaks? What about next summer? Would he want her here the whole time?

Missy had never been apart from her daughter for more than a few weeks, and knowing Casey would be here in Destiny with Liam while Missy was back in England would be a tough pill to swallow.

"Hey, where'd you go?"

She blinked, his words causing the empty plate in front of her to come back into focus. "Oh, sorry. I got lost there for a moment." She looked at him now, hoping her smile appeared easier than it felt. "I blame the wine."

He reached for the bottle of merlot, the second one they'd opened, and filled her almost empty glass again. "No sense in letting it go to waste."

"It's a good thing neither one of us has to drive home."

His hand stilled for a moment before he emptied the remains of the bottle into his own glass. "Yes, a good thing.

Just like this dinner. Thank you for rescuing me from my cooking calamity tonight."

"I'd like to think tonight was a joint effort."

Liam smiled and lifted his glass. "Here's to working well together."

Missy lifted hers and they gently clinked them before each took another sip.

"Why don't you go and enjoy the rest of your wine in front of the fire," Liam said, "while I clean up in here."

"You don't want help?"

He got to his feet, shaking his head. "I'm going to let the dishes soak in the sink. I'll join you in a minute."

Missy rose as well, automatically reaching for her plate, but Liam got there first. She returned his smile and headed for the living room, taking her glass with her.

Walking around the room, she let her fingers trail over the soft leather of the love seat before settling on the matching couch. She noticed that like the rest of the house, this room was beautifully put together. The furniture, lamps and art worked well together, masculine in style with rich earth-tone colors that fit Liam's personality and the ruggedness of the log home. Still, the place needed a hint of something soft as well as brightening—

"Hey, you're frowning," Liam said, coming in from the kitchen. "What are you thinking so hard about?"

She offered another smile. "Your place. It's lovely."

"You can thank my mom and Katie. It was only finished this summer, and I was so busy I gave them free rein when it came to getting the main rooms done." He joined her on the couch. "But your frown tells me your designer's eye has found something wrong."

"Not wrong," she said, looking around again. "But a few things might make it more personal. More you."

"Like what?"

"Maybe a cerulean-blue cashmere throw, some golden sandstone-colored pillows, a plant or two." The list rolled off her tongue as she easily pictured the items in selected spots. "A favorite book or two for the tables and a few family photos..."

Her voice faded when her gaze caught on the grouping of simple black frames centered on the fireplace mantel.

Unable to stop herself, she placed her glass on the large square coffee table and rose, drawn by the photographs of her and Casey. And Liam.

One was of him and Casey, smiling, heads tucked in close, their faces filling the frame. Another was of her and Casey sitting next to each other on the dock, talking, their feet dangling in the lake.

There was Casey playing the guitar, not even aware of the picture being taken, and the smallest frame held an old black-and-white photo of Missy and Liam taken years ago. Dirty from a rodeo competition, Liam stood, grinning, a trophy held aloft in one arm while the other was wrapped around her, holding her close to his side. Her head was tipped back at she stared at him in utter adulation.

"When did you—how did you—"

The fact that he had photographs of her—of all of them—so prominently displayed threatened to take her strength. She grabbed onto the mantel. How had she missed seeing these when she'd first walked in tonight and just now, as she'd analyzed the decor of this room?

"Hey, are you okay?" He left the couch and stood in front of her, one hand touching her shoulder. "Missy?"

She shook her head, gulped in a deep breath and some-how found her voice. "I'm sorry. These—the pictures surprised me, that's all. When did you do this?"

"Just last week." He reached for the frame that held the image of him and Casey. "She took this one of us on Sunday morning and sent it to me. I printed it out, and later that day—I think you were in the kitchen or something—she helped me pick out the others, and we found a few frames in the main house for them."

"And this one?"

Liam put the first frame back in its place. His mouth softened, his lips hiking at one corner as he reached for the old photograph of the two of them. "Casey spotted this when I showed her our old senior yearbook. I remembered how I snuck into the graphic arts room at the high school and *acquired* the actual photograph after you and I had... well, the September after you returned home."

His story surprised her. "You did?"

"Took me a couple of days of searching through my old stuff to find it. I thought I'd give it to Casey. She got such a kick out of seeing us as teenagers."

Trying desperately not to get caught up in a haze of memories from years past mixed with the moments they'd spent together over the last weeks, Missy took a step back. Then another, needing space between her and Liam before she did something stupid.

Like throw herself into his arms.

She blinked away the image, noticing for the first time the long envelope tucked in behind the picture frames, the return address for the genetic testing center in the upper corner.

"What is that?"

Liam returned the picture to the mantel and retrieved the envelope. "*This* is the reason I asked you and Casey to dinner tonight."

"The DNA results?"

He nodded.

"But it's not opened."

"Nope."

Understanding dawned. "You were planning to open it tonight, while the three of us were here together."

This time he shook his head, his gaze on the packet as he turned it over repeatedly in his hands. "No, actually I planned to toss it into the fire."

She gasped. "What?"

"I don't need to see in black and white what I know in my heart—what I've known from the moment she told me—to be true." He looked at Missy then, genuine certainty in his blue eyes. "She is a part of me, a part of us. Casey is my daughter."

A warmth that had nothing to do with the fire radiated throughout Missy's body. A sharp sting soon had her vision wavering and she had to close her eyes, but a tear escaped anyway.

"Hey, what's this for?" Liam whispered, his hand cupping her cheek, his thumb brushing the moisture away.

"That's—" her voice broke and she had to swallow hard before she could continue "—the first time you've said that."

"Huh?"

She opened her eyes, her smile wobbly as she took in his puzzled expression. "Tonight, right now, is the first time you've actually said Casey is your daughter."

"No."

Missy nodded. "At least to me, and you've never said it directly to Casey. Believe me, she's been waiting."

This time it was Liam who closed his eyes, dropping his hand from Missy's face as he turned away. "Are you kidding me? Damn, could I be any more stupid?"

"Hey, you're not—"

"I could've sworn I've told her." He cut her off and pressed his fist with the crumbled results against his chest.

"I know it in my head. I feel it in my heart. I have from the beginning."

She believed him. She could see it on his face, hear it in his words, and her own doubts about him accepting her story as the truth released their last hold on her. "I think when you insisted on the test…"

"It was the first thing that popped into my head that night on the porch. To keep both of you here longer than a weekend." He dropped his hand, the paperwork inches from the flames. "I'm getting rid of this—"

"No!" She grabbed his wrist, stopping him. For good measure, she tugged the envelope from his fingers, pressing it to her chest as she backed up a few steps. "No, don't do that."

"Missy—"

"I know you believe." She moved back farther when he headed for her, stopping only when she felt the couch at the back of her legs. "You believe in me, believe in her, and that means everything…to both of us, but this is tangible proof. We'll need this paperwork in order to change her birth certificate."

"Change…" This time it was Liam's face that registered his shock, his voice gone as he stumbled past her and sank into the cushions. "Are you serious? You would do that? For me?"

Missy joined him, setting the test results on the table, so that she could take his hand in hers. "Casey is your daughter. Our daughter. Your name deserves to be on her birth certificate."

Chapter Twelve

Her words froze him in place, but at the same time Liam felt as if he were flying. The last thing he'd ever thought he would hear Missy say was that his name should be on Casey's birth certificate.

Would that change her last name, too?

He didn't have any idea how that worked, especially in the UK, but in this day and age, a name change was probably a separate action requiring more paperwork. Was that something Casey would be interested in?

The idea of her being a Murphy by name caused his chest to swell, but that would mean her last name and her mother's wouldn't be the same anymore. Unless Missy would consider—

"Liam?"

The way she whispered his name sent a flash of hot need racing through his veins. Then he noticed how tightly he was squeezing her hand and realized that she was just trying to get free from his grasp.

He eased his hold but didn't let go. Instead, he cradled her hand in both of his and gently rubbed her fingers. "Sorry. I didn't mean to hurt you."

"You didn't." Her lips curved in a gentle smile. "I surprised you."

The back of his throat burned, a sensation that quickly made its way upward as his eyes moistened. "I'm stunned. Flabbergasted."

She rested her free hand against his cheek. "I can see that."

Right here, right now, he wanted nothing more than to haul her into his arms. He wouldn't do it, of course. As astounded as he was over how this night was going—from the burned dinner to this startling conversation—he suddenly couldn't think about anything else other than kissing her.

Kissing her and holding her and making love with her.

The last three times they'd kissed, she'd been willing, but he'd been the one to make the first move. Even when she had practically come right out and asked him to.

This time, it had to be from her.

He could see the longing in her eyes, feel it in her touch. Swallowing hard, he stared at her.

Please, Missy, please come to me.

She leaned forward, bringing their bodies closer, hesitating when her breasts brushed against his arm.

Forcing himself to stay completely still, he kept his gaze on her as she inched closer again, her fingers tightening around his this time. But she stopped when her lips were a hairbreadth away from his.

He didn't close his eyes as he bowed to the slight pressure of her fingers against his jaw, allowing Missy to bring his mouth to hers. Her initial kisses were cautious. As if they were kissing for the first time, both with their eyes wide-open, innocent and unsure. Her soft, sweet breath was warm against his mouth and his muscles hardened everywhere when he refused to let his body do what it wanted.

She pressed her mouth to his more firmly, and then he felt the tip of her tongue trace the edge of his bottom lip. A low growl escaped his throat. Her eyelids closed, but not before he saw the victorious flash in those blue depths.

He tunneled his fingers into her hair, tipping her head back as he claimed her, opening his mouth to welcome her in.

Releasing him, she grabbed at his shoulders as he pulled her onto his lap and sank back into the leather cushions, their kisses growing hotter, wetter and frantic.

It wasn't enough. Wasn't nearly enough.

Both hands at her waist now, he lifted her while stretching out completely on the oversize couch, fitting her perfectly against his body as she blanketed him.

"Oh!" she cried out as their mouths broke free and her hands landed on either side of his head.

"It's okay. I've got you," he whispered against her neck, before she drew back to look down at him. "I mean…is this okay?"

Her smile was like a liquid arrow straight to the part of him nestled against her. "It's very okay."

Two soft thuds caught his attention for a moment, but then the cool touch of her toes tangling with his bare feet felt as intimate as if they were lying here totally naked.

Which wasn't a bad idea. But for now, he wanted her like this.

Lifting his head, he placed his lips just below her collarbone, nipping soft, wet bites as he moved south to the swell of her breasts. She rose up on her arms, scooting forward so that he could lie back down and still have her right where he needed her to be.

Her low moans filled the air as his hands reached beneath the edge of her top and traveled to the lacy cups of her bra.

He nosed the neckline off one shoulder at the same moment his hand peeled away the delicate material covering her. As he sucked her nipple into his mouth, she arched against him, rotating her pelvis as instinct took over. The heat of her melted through her skirt and his shirt, reminding him how long it'd been since he'd made love to a woman.

This woman.

No one else mattered except her.

No one ever would.

He released the tiny nub and started toward the other, but she slid down his body, crushing her mouth to him again in a rush of wild kisses. Her fingers were just as busy at the buttons on his shirt and soon she had it opened almost to his waist.

Pushing the material to one side, she released his mouth and pressed hot, openmouthed kisses down his throat and across his chest. Over his heart. She traced the outer edge of his tattoo with the tip of her tongue, leaving behind wet heat as she neared his left shoulder.

"Missy…"

"Am I hurting you?"

Yeah, she was killing him, but that's not what she was asking. "No, but you don't have to—"

"I want to."

Her words were whispered against his skin, but still, he reached for her. She grabbed his hand and pushed it up and back until it was shackled beside his head by her fingers. Breaking free of her hold would have been easy, but he let her keep him there as her mouth danced lightly over the puckered scar tissue.

He groaned, loving the feel of her lips on him there and wanting her to do the same to him everywhere. But the way she was moving against him, hip to hip now, was going to end things before they even began.

He broke free and rose up on one elbow, opening his legs wide. Capturing her between them, he squeezed. "Missy, wait."

Her kisses continued as she scooted farther down his chest. "Don't want to."

Hell, he loved hearing her say that. "I'm not going to… last. And I'd rather we continued this in a bed. My bed."

She looked up at him, her chin resting high on his stomach. Bright pink highlighted her already flushed features. "Do you remember the last time we did it in a bed?"

He chuckled at the memory and flopped back down to the couch. "You mean the only time? You lied to your host family, I lied to my folks and we snuck off to that shabby motel on the outskirts of Cheyenne the weekend before graduation."

She crawled back up his body until they were face-to-face again. "We were so nervous about getting caught."

"Yeah, until we weren't."

Nodding, she looked away, her eyes taking on a faraway expression. "You know… I was going to tell you that night. About the plans I'd made to stay in Wyoming. Go to school here."

His smile faded as he looked up at her, wanting nothing more than to tighten his arms around her. Instead, he kept his hands loose at her waist. "Why didn't you?"

"I was still waiting on the final word about getting money out of my trust. Without that, there was no way I could afford it, but I think now that was just an excuse."

She hitched her shoulders in a tiny shrug and looked back at him. "You were so excited about high school being over in a few days. The entire summer was already planned when it came to your rodeo competitions."

The hurt in her voice, even after all these years, tugged at him. He brushed a strand of her hair from her cheek. "Plans for us. Plans to be together."

"Plans for your future." She looked at him again. "I should have known something was up when I couldn't get you to talk about going to college in the fall."

"I can't say that rodeoing full-time hadn't crossed my mind. Heck, it'd been a dream since I was a kid, but I didn't want to think about packing off to college mainly because you were going to be gone by then."

Missy nodded and he could almost see her turning over his words in her head. He couldn't believe how fast they'd gone from being on the brink of making love to talking about the past.

It was the future that he was interested in, especially when it came to where they were headed tonight.

"I want you to stay," he said, "but if you'd rather not…"

Her breath hitched. "Stay?"

"Here, tonight." Didn't she understand what he was saying? "With me."

Silence stretched between them for a long moment. So long, he was convinced she was going to turn him down. But then she said, "I want that, too."

His heart raced again at her words. He wanted nothing more than to grab her and head upstairs, but first things first.

"Ah, can you give me a few minutes?" he asked.

Confusion filled her eyes. "For…"

"I wasn't expecting this. I mean, I'd hoped—okay, fantasized about you and me being together, but I didn't want to…"

"Jinx anything?" she said when his voice faded.

"Exactly. And I didn't want to presume."

He returned her smile, and gently easing her off his body, moved to the edge of the couch. "So I need to check the upstairs. Light a few candles. Make sure I don't have any dirty socks thrown around. That kind of thing. I'll be right back."

"That's what you said earlier."

He remembered. "And you said you'd be here."

"Do I have to say it again?"

Yes, she did. He wanted her promise that she wasn't going to change her mind. But deep inside, he knew if at any point she decided that being with him wasn't what she wanted, he'd let her go.

It might kill him, but he'd do it.

She cupped his face, pressing her lips to his in a quick kiss. "I'll be here."

As much as he hated to, he turned away.

Straightening took a bit of effort, considering his condition, but he headed for the kitchen. There were emergency pillar candles in the pantry. Not purchased for an occasion like this, but it was the best he could do on short notice. He grabbed a few, a couple of drinking glasses to use as holders and a box of matches.

Then he remembered the trio of vintage Old West–style oil lamps on the fireplace mantel in his room. Katie had teased him about how he'd be all set if the power ever went out or he had a lady friend stay the night.

"Not just a friend," he whispered to himself. "More like the love of your life."

He started to leave, but then turned back and grabbed the vase filled with roses off the table. Heading down the side hall by his office, he paused when he got back to the foyer, glanced into the living room and found Missy sitting up, facing the fire, wineglass in hand.

Taking the stairs two at a time, he prayed she wasn't having second thoughts.

Was she doing the right thing?

This evening had already been so amazing. Finding Liam fretting over his attempts at cooking had eased her nervousness, and just the two of them sharing a meal and talking about everyday things had felt...familiar, comfortable, with a hint of something simmering between them at the edges.

Something that exploded once she'd made it clear to him what she wanted this time. She wanted Liam. Wanted the two of them to have this night together.

Not that she would have deliberately tried to create a chance like this, despite her feelings for the man. Their lives were too different; they lived on two different continents, for goodness' sake.

But for whatever reason, events had conspired to bring them to this moment. No strings, no plans. No thoughts about anything or anyone outside the warm timbered walls of his spectacular home.

How could she walk away from this?

A single yellow rose appeared before her and she jumped when it brushed her cheek. Then she tipped her head back and found Liam standing behind her, leaning over the back of the sofa.

"I called your name. You must've been lost in thought."

"I was."

"Good thoughts, I hope." He held out his hand.

She stood up, set her empty glass on the table and

walked to him, lacing her fingers with his. "Very good thoughts."

He smiled and stepped backward into the foyer. She followed, her breath catching at the sight of rose petals scattered on the stairs. "Oh, Liam. How sweet. You didn't have to do that."

"Yeah, I did."

He pulled her into his arms and drew her close. The kiss was soft and gentle, but only for a moment. Then that hunger returned as she became aware of him, his strength and the urgency in his hold when the most intimate part of him pressed against her.

He released her but kept one of her hands in his. He started up the stairs. She kept pace, the petals cool beneath her feet. At the top, she smiled at the trail continuing down the hall and into his bedroom, where more surprises waited. A wash of candlelight filled the space. On his dresser, the bedside tables, the rough-hewn beam that served as the fireplace mantel, sat glowing lanterns and candles. Soft instrumental music came from an unseen source and rose petals decorated his king-size bed.

She flattened her hand to her chest; the wild beating of her heart matched the speed with which she blinked, fighting back tears. "Liam, this is so beautiful."

"You're beautiful." He turned her to him, taking her face in his hands, and gently kissed her lips, her cheeks, along her jaw and just below her ear. "*You* are so beautiful," he repeated, the lightest whisper into her hair. "And I'm so happy you and I are finally here, together, like this."

She reached for him, popping the last button on his shirt. Desperate to feel the heat of his skin against hers, she pushed the soft material from his shoulders, forcing him to let her go so that she could rid him of the clothing entirely. After his shirt fell to the floor, her fingers lightly danced over his skin, over the beautiful tattoo that represented the heart of this man.

Strong, determined, courageous.

She laid a hand there, barely covering the intricate tattoo, loving that his heart was pounding out a cadence that matched hers.

Looking up and finding him watching her with a slow, sexy smile set off a wave of need and desire inside her. She reached for the bottom edge of her shirt, but he gripped her hands, stopping her.

"Let me."

Lifting her hands high over her head, she kept them there as he eased off her top. Once it was gone, she lowered her arms, but he had his fingers in her hair.

"Can you please take this down?" he asked. "I love it when it's loose and flowing over your shoulders."

With the removal of a few pins, it was done. He found the simple elastic waistband of her skirt and slid it easily over her legs until it pooled at her feet, pausing to leave an openmouthed kiss on the scrap of lace that rode high on her hips before he eased her panties from her body as well.

"Hey, you've got a scar of your own." His fingers lightly traced the thin line that ran low on her abdomen.

Sending a silent thank-you for years of yoga classes, she still constricted her stomach muscles and tried not to squirm under his close inspection. "Yes, but mine's only fifteen years old."

He looked up, understanding in his eyes. "You had Casey via cesarean?"

She nodded. "I was quite a bit tinier back then, and she was just over nine pounds when she was born."

Keeping his gaze locked with hers, Liam leaned in and placed his lips over the faded blemish, leaving a trail of kisses that brought tears to her eyes.

When he dropped his head lower, his mouth and tongue loving her where she throbbed, she tunneled her fingers into his hair, holding him there as she spiraled up and out of control. When she came, she cried out.

He rose, swearing under his breath, both of them reaching behind her to unhook her bra. Their hands tangled before she brushed him away to pull the straps from her shoulders. Raw, naked desire filled his gaze, causing her breasts to tingle, her nipples to harden all over again.

He yanked her into his arms, and they were finally skin to skin, as their mouths came together in heated, devouring kisses. Grabbing at his waist, her fingers fumbled with the edge of his jeans. She managed to get the top button undone, but it wasn't enough, especially when she could feel the hard length of him pressing against her belly.

Missy gasped, tearing her mouth from his. "Jeans. Off. Now."

"Hmm, where has my proper little English lass gone?" Liam teased.

"She's right here. Wanting desperately to make love to you."

A low growl filled his chest as he stepped back, ridding himself of his jeans and boxer briefs at the same time. His body was perfection and she wanted to feel him against her desperately. She reached out to touch him, but he took her hand, bringing her around to the side of the bed. With his free hand, he yanked back the dark blue comforter, sending rose petals flying in the air, and Missy couldn't help but giggle at the sight.

Seconds later, he had her flat on her back, pinned beneath his hard body as he kissed her, his hands roaming over her, reigniting her arousal all over again. She cupped him in her hand, loving his moan as she caressed him while he, in turn, lavished attention on her breasts with his lips, his fingers slicking across the most sensitive part of her.

"Ah, you are so wet," he rasped against her throat. "Wet for me."

"Yes, thanks to you. *Liam, please...*"

He rolled away from her then, reaching for the drawer on the bedside table. She debated telling him that wasn't necessary. She was on birth control and her last steady relationship had ended three years ago. She was healthy, but she had no idea when he'd last been physically intimate with someone.

He sat back on his knees, put on the protection and then moved between her open legs. "It's been a while...since I've done this. I'm not going to last long this first time."

"It's been a while for me, too," she confessed, thrilled at his words. Then she caught what he'd said. "First time?"

"Oh, yeah." He grinned, but then his smile slipped a bit as he looked down at her, an unspoken question in his gaze.

"It's been a few years," she said.

"I don't want to hurt you."

She wrapped her hands around his waist, pulling him closer until she felt him right where she wanted him. "You won't."

Still, he went slowly, a tremble coursing over his muscles as he eased inside. She was tight, but arching her body, she opened, making room for him as she rose up to meet his kiss.

When he was finally deep inside her, he broke free from her mouth, tucking his head next to hers, his lips at her neck. "You...okay?" His words were guttural and strained.

She tightened her hold on him. "I'm wonderful."

"Ah, Missy..."

Proving it, she rocked her hips, urging him to move as well, and he did. He reached one hand beneath her, cupping her backside as he lifted her, giving her more and more, meeting her thrusts with his own until her entire body tightened and she clung to him and shattered.

He followed, repeating her name again and again as he found his own release before covering her body with his. Joy filled her. She'd gotten what she'd wanted, but everything was now changed.

She was in love. And scared to death.

So scared, Missy tiptoed around Liam's bedroom, getting dressed with the hope of not waking him after an incredible night. She hadn't planned on sleeping over, but whenever she mentioned going back to the boathouse he'd kiss her, and before she knew it they were making passionate love again.

At some point, he'd gotten out of bed, extinguished the candles and lanterns and gone downstairs to make sure the fire was out as well. He'd come back with her phone, the two-way radio and a crystal decanter of ice water and glasses, smiling indulgently as she'd checked to see if she had any text messages from their daughter, which of course she didn't.

She'd then clicked on the email button, noticing her inbox was full to bursting, but Liam had relieved her of her phone and proceeded to make her forget about anything outside the cozy confines of his bedroom, time and time again.

So thoughtful, so loving, so—

No. She had to put a stop to her crazy and out-of-control emotions before she started to believe what she felt meant anything.

It didn't. It couldn't.

The last month had been a world of make-believe for her and for Casey. Missy had put their lives on hold because of the amazing truth she'd found out, but in a week the fantasy was coming to an end. She would go back to her life, Liam would go back to his and somehow they'd find a way to make it work for their daughter's sake.

"Hey, what are you doing?"

His rough, sleep-filled voice stilled her hands as she attempted to make order of her messy hair.

"Getting dressed," she said, stating the obvious before glancing his way in time to watch him roll onto his back. The sheets tightened across his lower half, highlighting his washboard abs and an impressive morning erection that reminded her of all the wonderful things they'd done last night.

"Why?" he asked, rubbing at his eyes.

She blinked and forced herself to look away. "I should head back to the boathouse. Someone might—"

He dropped his hand, his gaze focused now. "Casey won't be back for another day and a half."

"Your mother?"

"She usually doesn't show up this early uninvited."

Missy waved at the bright sunshine pouring in through the windows. "It's almost nine o'clock."

"Why are you running away when we have so much to talk about?"

His question caused her heart to race. "We do?"

"Of course." He yawned and pushed into a sitting position, stopping suddenly when things got a bit uncomfortable, she guessed, but then he bent one knee and tugged the sheet back over his lap. "We need to make plans. For the future. For getting you and Casey in Destiny on a permanent basis."

Shocked filled her. "What?"

"I know this is kind of sudden, but I want you here, both of you." He leaned forward. "You said you were here on a work visa. How long is that good for? And Casey is half American. We'll need to find out how we can get her dual citizenship. You said your company has offices in LA, but you do most of your design work from home and you can travel whenever you need to. Casey loves it here and I know she'll be happy—"

"Wait just a bloody minute!" Missy held up a hand, cutting him off. How could he make assumptions like that? "I can't just up and move to America! My home, my career, my mother—despite our current relationship—are back in London. My *life* is in London. So is Casey's with her friends and her school."

"She has friends and school here. Family, too, and her father. I'm just trying to figure out a plan—"

"Blast it, it's like nothing has changed." Missy reeled from his words. "You're doing the same thing you did years ago. Making plans based on your needs and wants. You've always had that luxury, but that's not how being a parent works."

She paced the area at the end of his bed. "If it was just me...if I only had myself to think about, I might be temp—" She cut off her words, refusing to allow her emotions to get in the way. "I can't uproot my life, and my daughter's, because you and I rekindled a teenage passion into one night of great sex."

One night? Liam had just experienced the most amazing night with the woman he loved—the only woman he'd ever truly loved—and she was calling what they shared a fling?

Being with her had been a dream come true, every moment of it, and long after she'd fallen asleep in his arms in the wee hours of the morning, he'd started—well, making plans.

The last thing he'd expected was this reaction or for

her to throw his immature behavior from sixteen years ago back in his face. This wasn't like then. He wasn't the same person. He had responsibilities that went far beyond himself or even his family.

"Missy, I'm the CEO and president of my family's company. I can't just move to another continent—"

"Exactly. No one is asking you to. Or telling you to, for that matter."

"That's not what I'm doing."

"Really?" She folded her arms across her chest. "That's what it sounds like to me."

He opened his mouth to set her straight on a few things—most importantly, how he felt about her and their daughter—but the two-way radio on the bedside table chirped, and then Nolan's voice came over the airwaves.

"Liam? Come in, Liam. You there?"

Damn! This was the last thing he needed right now. Leaning back, he grabbed the radio, pressing the receive button. "Yeah, I'm here. What's up?"

"Casey's missing."

Missy's gasp filled the air, and Liam's stomach fell to his feet. He reached for her with his free hand, but she shook her head and stayed where she was, panic now etched on her face.

"What do you mean missing?" Liam asked.

"She and Abby got up early…took a couple of the ATVs to the ridge to watch the sunrise. According to Abby they had…words, and Casey told her she was going back." Nolan's voice broke, static marring his description. "Abby thought she meant the cabin, but by the time she returned, Casey still hadn't shown up."

"You're out looking for her now." It was a statement, not a question. Liam knew his brother well. "Where are you?"

"I've been doubling back on the three possible trails, but

you know as well as I do how many offshoots they have. I haven't found her. I'm thinking if she stayed on the main road, she'd be back to the house by now. Have you seen her this morning?"

Liam got out of bed, radio in hand as he reached for the clothes he'd tossed on a nearby chair at some point during the night, but Missy was already gone. His front door slammed as she raced outside, yelling their daughter's name.

His heart froze when he heard nothing in response.

Chapter Thirteen

She had to be out here. Somewhere. It was almost noon, just after their self-imposed two-hour search deadline, and no one had found Casey.

Liam rode the all-terrain vehicle along the trails, moving slowly as he searched the dense forest. He could hear the company's helicopter overhead and knew Bryant was doing what he could from the air, while Adam and his dad were on horseback, taking the less-used road from Adam's property, with Fay staying behind just in case Casey somehow found her way there.

Nolan worked the trail that led farther up into the mountains, and Abby and the twins stayed at the cabin if she returned. His mom and Laurie had the formidable task of keeping Missy calm back at the main house. She'd only agreed to stay behind when Liam reminded her that Casey might get past him and make her way home.

Find my daughter.

Missy's parting words this morning had cut deep. Liam had wanted to point out that Casey was *their* daughter, but the pain and fear in Missy's eyes had held him back from saying or doing anything, other than laying a hard kiss on her mouth and promising to bring Casey home.

Concentrating on the search helped a little, but his mind still replayed the argument he and Missy had had this morning. Where had he gone wrong? He wanted them in his life, wanted them in Destiny. He'd been so sure Missy felt the same way. To hear her say differently tore at his heart.

After finishing a trek on a rarely used dead-end trail deep in the woods, he pulled to the side of the road and let the vehicle idle. Then he checked in with everyone at the twenty-minute interval they'd agreed on. Still nothing. His last transmission was to Missy, as he'd insisted no one contact her but him. He didn't want a million voices coming at her with the same bleak news.

"Missy, it's Liam." He didn't waste any words. "We're still looking."

A long pause filled the air, but the static told him she was there. "It's been two hours," she finally said. "Where could she be?"

He wished he knew.

Wiping the sweat from his brow, Liam pressed the talk button. "We'll find her."

"She must be hurt. I keep trying her cell phone, but... she wouldn't ignore my texts. She just wouldn't. I can't bear to think of her lying somewhere...alone."

The heartbreak in Missy's tone had Liam fisting his hand and jamming it into his thigh. Missing the mark, he hit the ATV's kill switch instead, shutting the machine down. Dammit! As he blinked hard, the woods turned into watery shades of green and brown and silence enveloped him.

He swallowed a few times before he trusted himself to talk. "I think we should—"

A faint noise, a mechanical whine, carried on the breeze, stopping him cold. He lowered the radio and, concentrated on the sound, wanting to be sure. Yes, that was man-made. It had to be.

"Liam?" Missy's voice came back. "Why did—"

"Give me a minute. I think I heard something."

Missy's gasp filled the air, but she remained silent. He climbed off the ATV and hurried to the side of the road he'd avoided, due to the soft mud and the steep decline into a gully.

No tracks, at least not at this end.

He stood still, straining to hear—yes, there it was again. Heading back up the way he'd just come, he walked farther into the woods, peering down into the dark undergrowth filled with fallen logs and shrubbery so thick the filtered sunlight bounced off it.

"Casey!" He called out. "Sweetie, can you hear me?"

Something—instinct, awareness, a father's love—called to him now in a way that it hadn't before. She was here, she was close.

He tried again. "Casey, where are you?"

Then he saw it—a rear wheel, spinning upside down in the greenery, the rest of the vehicle barely visible in the dense woods.

His heart vaulted into his throat. "Casey! It's Dad! Are you okay? Can you answer me?"

A long moment passed and he searched for a way down to where the ATV lay, his boots catching and sliding in the sodden earth. Then a few feet away, a dark glove rose into a patch of sunlight, and stayed suspended there for a moment before it disappeared again.

"I see you! I'll be right there. Hang on!"

Liam reached for the closest tree branch, broke it into three pieces to form an arrow and laid it in the road. Racing back to his ATV, he grabbed a coil of rope and the emergency backpack, thumbing the button on the radio. "I found her!"

"Oh, Liam!" Relief flooded Missy's voice. "Is she okay? Is she hurt?"

"I don't know. I'm heading there now."

"Did she call out to you?"

"She only responded with a wave when I yelled. Probably due to her helmet." He prayed it was her gear that kept her silent. "Tell everyone I'm on the main trail, at the second fork from the mountain base. About two hundred yards in. I marked the spot on the road. There's a steep ravine on the left. She's down there."

"Oh, my God."

"Tell Nolan to take care of his kids, but send Adam and my dad this way in case I need help hauling her out of there." He started back up the road. "Have Bryant land, but keep the helo live...we might need to get her medical care in a hurry."

"Liam—"

"Do it, Missy. I have to sign off. I'll need both hands to get to her." He regretted his harsh tone, but he didn't have time to spare. "Let me bring our daughter home."

"Please, as soon as you can...call me back."

He promised and then pocketed the radio. Reaching the marker he'd left, he easily spotted the overturned ATV this time. He slung the backpack over his shoulder, tied one end of the rope to a tree, tossed the rest into the foliage below and started downward.

"Hang on, Casey," he yelled. "I'm coming."

It seemed to take forever to get to her. He kept a running commentary so that she'd know he was there, but honestly it was probably more to keep himself from falling to pieces. Finally, he reached her. She was laid out flat on her back next to a fallen tree that completely blocked her from the road.

Kneeling, he almost lost it again when he saw her staring at him through the cracked shield of the helmet. "I know I've been asking this for the last twenty minutes," he said, "but are you okay?"

She started to nod and then stopped, grimaced and mouthed something.

He lifted the shield, hating the tear tracks that stained her cheeks. "What is it, sweetie?"

"God, I'm a stupid wanker." Her words came out in a rough whisper. "I'm okay, but I ache from my teeth to my toes."

"Anywhere specific?" He leaned back, wondering what that fall must've been like and if she'd broken anything. "Any part of you that you can't move?"

"Everything seems to be working, except my right arm hurts bloody awful. Is Mum furious?"

Liam noticed that Casey was cradling her arm against her chest, the protective glove missing. She had a long-sleeved jacket on, but he could see her wrist was swollen badly, with dark color marring her skin. "Not furious. Worried. Just like the rest of us. That's some bruise you've got there."

"It's from an earlier tumble," she said. "Before I got myself into this mess. How did you know where to find me?"

"We've been looking for you all morning. Abby told us you took off after the two of you drove up to the ridge for the sunrise."

Casey's mouth pressed into a hard line, her eyes going cold. "Is that all she told you?"

A feeling of dread came over Liam. "What else is there?"

"We argued, got into a tussle." His daughter's words came out cool and collected, but he heard anger in her tone. "I landed hard against the rocks, banged up my wrist, but not before I landed a solid right hook to that pretty face."

Surprised filled him, but now wasn't the time to go into details of whatever had been brewing between the two girls. "Why don't you tell me about that later? I want to concentrate on getting you out of here."

"Come to my rescue again, huh?" Casey offered a half-hearted smile. "Bit more trouble than a blister this time."

Leaning in close, Liam brushed away a new tear from her cheek. "I'll always come to your rescue, sweetie. You're my daughter. That's what dads do."

Her eyes widened. "You…you truly believe that? Even without the test results?"

Now wasn't the time to reveal that he had the results or how badly he'd screwed things up this morning with his plans for the future. Thank goodness he still had a week to convince Missy the three of them belonged together.

"Yes, I believe that." He reached for her uninjured hand, his heart skipping a beat when she clung to him. "I knew from the beginning. I'm sorry I didn't make that clear to you. I love you, Casey. You're my daughter and I love you."

Every time the doctor touched Casey's arm, she winced despite the pain medication she'd been given and Missy's heart broke a bit more.

"As I suspected, you've got a couple of hairline fractures in the radius bone, located just above your wrist." The doctor laid Casey's arm gently back down on the gurney. "We're going to put you in a fiberglass cast."

"Really?" Casey asked. "For how long?"

"Minimum four weeks, maybe six. You're young. You'll heal nicely."

That would put them almost at Halloween, and of course, she and Casey would be back in London long before that. Wondering if there might be an issue, Missy opened her mouth, but Casey spoke up first.

"Can I travel? I mean, this won't stop me from flying, will it?"

Liam's head jerked up at their daughter's questions. Missy could see why. Casey sounded anxious, even eager to leave.

He sat on the other side of the room, having given up his spot at Casey's bedside when the doctor came back with the X-rays.

Except for explaining to the staff, and the sheriff, who happened to be at the clinic, what happened today, Liam had remained silent as Missy spoke about Casey's medical history and answered what seemed like a thousand questions.

"No, you should be fine," the doctor said. "I'd recommend taking along a pillow to keep it elevated. Now, let's get you fixed up, and yes, your mother can come with you."

Casey nodded, her gaze straight ahead and her brows furrowed in a way that was so familiar, Missy realized it was the same expression Liam often used. In fact, he had the matching look on his face right now.

What was he thinking? Was he upset that the doctor hadn't invited him along as well?

He'd been so calm when they arrived at the main house, Casey riding in front of him. Other than a quick hug and a fevered thank-you, they'd barely spoken to each other in the ensuing chaos.

Was it just this morning that she'd awoken in his arms?

"Mum? You ready?"

Missy started, realizing Casey and the doctor were waiting on her. "Yes. Of course." She looked at Liam again and decided to say what the doctor hadn't. "Do you want to—"

"I'll stay here," he said, cutting her off. "It'll be too crowded. Besides, there's paperwork to be taken care of."

"I have health insurance."

He got to his feet, something heartbreakingly haggard in his expression. "Don't worry about it."

"Liam—"

"Just take care of Casey, okay?" He walked over and laid a hand on their daughter's leg, below her knee and far away from her injured wrist. "I'm glad you weren't hurt even worse. You gave all of us quite a scare."

"Well, thank you. For saving me."

Liam gave a quick nod and then stepped away.

Missy was amazed at how they were acting toward each other. It was as if the closeness they'd found over the last five weeks had disappeared.

This was not the same man who'd had tears in his eyes when he spoke last night about knowing in his heart Casey was his daughter.

Or the one who'd passionately stated his case this morning for having her—both of them—move to Destiny. Now was not the time to talk about that, but they needed to soon. Missy hoped they'd find a chance. For everyone's sake.

In less than an hour, Missy had the pain medication in her purse and Casey sported a bright pink cast on her right arm. Liam stood when they walked into the waiting area, but when they headed out to the parking lot, Casey switched sides so that it was Missy's hand she held tight.

Missy could see her daughter was exhausted and still in pain. Getting her back to the boathouse and into bed was the best thing—

"Casey!"

The three of them stopped and turned. Casey's grip tightened as Nathan Lawson jogged toward them. Missy glanced at Liam, not liking the way his eyes narrowed on the young man.

"What's he doing?" Casey started to say, and then stopped and addressed the boy directly when he joined them. "What are you doing here?"

"I heard about your accident."

Casey turned to her, rolling her eyes. "Bugger, this is a small town."

"Actually, my mom works at the clinic. Are you okay?"

Casey waved her cast-covered arm at him and then winced.

"Ah, yeah, that was a stupid question." Nathan's gaze flew between Missy and Liam, but since her daughter hadn't let go of her, Missy wasn't going anywhere. Neither was Liam, from the stormy look on his face.

Quickly figuring out he wasn't going to get her alone, Nathan continued, "Look, I'm happy we got things straight between us last night."

"Last night?" Liam asked, before Missy could.

"Yes, sir. I knew Casey was up at your family's cabin, but it seems her cell phone gets reception there. We texted and I explained about what she saw at school yesterday. Or what she thought she saw."

"What Abby *told* me I was seeing," Casey said, her words spoken with a bitter tone. "She's your ex-girlfriend, she's staying that way and she kissed you. Don't worry, Nathan, everything's fine."

The boy didn't look convinced, nor did he seem as if

he wanted to leave, but Missy's main concern was getting Casey home. "We should be heading back. Casey needs to rest."

"Right, sure." Nathan took a step back. "You're probably not going to want to hang out or anything this weekend, but I'll see you in school on Monday?"

"No, you won't. I'm going home. To London."

Shocked, Missy stared at her daughter. "Sweetie, we don't leave until next Monday. That's a week away."

Casey shook her head, her gaze rooted to the ground. "No, I want to go home. Now. Tomorrow. As soon as we can."

Silence filled the air. Missy sneaked a peek at Liam and the misery on his face at their daughter's declaration caused her stomach to clench.

He looked so lost and alone, even though he stood right here with them. Unlike this morning, when he'd looked ready to fight for his cause, now he appeared to have had the wind knocked out of him.

"Um, okay." Nathan took a few steps back, picking up on the tension. "I'm sorry to see you go. We'll stay in touch? Maybe you'll come back to Destiny for Christmas?"

Casey shrugged. "Maybe. I don't know."

Looking almost as dejected as Liam, the boy only nodded, said goodbye to all of them and turned and walked away.

Confused, Missy placed her fingertips beneath her daughter's chin and gently forced her to look up. "Hey, what's going on? Where did this come from?"

"Nowhere. I just want to go home."

"Because of what happened today?" Liam asked softly, drawing Missy's attention. "No one blames you, Casey, for any of it. It was an accident, that's all."

A tiny hiccup squeaked from Casey, and Missy looked back in time to see her daughter's eyes fill with tears.

"No, it's not…about the mess I caused. I'm glad we came here, glad we all know the truth, glad that we met." She spoke to Liam, but kept her back to him, her eyes pleading with Missy. "But I've had enough. I miss our home, my room, my school, my friends. I just want to go home. Please? Please, can we go home?"

Pulling her daughter gently to her, Missy tucked Casey's head beneath her chin and began swaying back and forth, an instinctive gesture of comfort instilled in her the first time they'd placed Casey in her arms as a wee babe.

Missy looked up, her heart breaking for the agony Liam was going through, but she'd been serious this morning when she'd told him that she couldn't just up and move her life—their lives—to Destiny.

Especially now, when she had to do what was best for her daughter. For their daughter.

"I'm taking her home."

Liam's world was falling apart and there was nothing he could do about it.

In the span of just over twenty-four hours, he'd gone from the high of being a man in love, overjoyed at the idea of making his claim to fatherhood official and planning for the future, to standing here at the security gates of the Cheyenne airport saying goodbye to the two women he loved most.

They'd returned from the clinic yesterday afternoon to a quiet homecoming as everyone stayed out of sight. Missy had gone to get Casey settled while he had the unhappy task of telling his family they were leaving, a full week ahead of schedule.

But first he'd had a talk with Abby.

She'd owned up to what had happened between her and Casey, even though Liam wasn't convinced he had the whole story. The side of Abby's face was swollen, and he was sure she'd have a souvenir from her English cousin that she wouldn't soon forget.

When he'd gathered everyone together in the main house, he'd explained what happened at the clinic, and Casey and Missy's decision to leave early, as best he could. He'd then tried to deal with their questions, most of which he didn't have any answers to.

Missy had shown up with the news that she'd been able to get them on a late-afternoon flight to New York and then a red-eye to London the next day. He'd insisted she upgrade their tickets to first class on his dime. He wanted Casey to be as comfortable as possible.

When she and Casey had said goodbye to everyone earlier, Missy had been gracious and kind, especially to his parents, which meant a lot to him. Casey had seemed genuinely upset about leaving and he'd kept hoping she'd announce she'd changed her mind and wanted to stay, even if it was only for the additional week, but now that they were at the airport, she looked excited about heading home.

And Missy? He couldn't quite figure out how she felt about all of this.

"Don't be mad at me."

Casey's softly spoken request yanked Liam from his thoughts. He looked at her, still amazed that this wondrous creature was now a part of his life.

"I could never be mad at you," he said.

"Only because you haven't known me that long." She smiled and he was glad to see the spark back in her eyes. "Just ask my mum."

Liam glanced at Missy, loving the all-encompassing

way she looked at their daughter and wishing desperately she'd look at him that way, too.

"Okay," he said, turning his attention back to his daughter. "How about I promise that I'm not mad about this?"

"Truly?"

He nodded, pushing the words past the lump in his throat. "I know I told you yesterday, but I'll keep saying it. I love you, Casey, and I only want what's best for you. You're the most important thing in my life and leaving doesn't change that fact."

"Oh, Dad, I love you, too!"

She flew at him and Liam caught her, taking care with her injury as he pulled her into his embrace.

He had to close his eyes, wanting to commit this moment—the first time she'd used the familiar moniker so many men took for granted—to memory, knowing he'd replay it over and over again in the coming days.

Opening his eyes again, he found Missy standing there, her fingers pressed to her lips and a bright sheen in her gaze as she watched them.

He gave Casey an extra squeeze before releasing her, and then reached inside his jean jacket and pulled out the stuffed buffalo he'd picked up at the gift shop while they'd been checking in. "Here's a new friend to keep you company on the plane."

"Oh, he's bloody cute!" Casey squealed and gave him another quick hug. "And he's the official state mammal for Wyoming. I love him, and I love you!"

She dropped to her knees, busying herself with finding room in her bag, allowing Liam to make his way to Missy.

"That was wonderful," she said when he stopped in front of her.

"It's just a stuffed toy."

"I was talking about what you said to our daughter… and when she called you Dad."

Damn, the lump in his throat was back and this time it matched the two-ton rock in his chest. "Yeah, I was pretty happy about that. Wasn't sure I was going to hear that before—well, I thought the first time might be via a text message."

Missy smiled, but the emotion didn't reach her eyes, which remained solemn. "Liam, we need to talk, to figure out—"

"We will, just not here. Not now."

He didn't wait for her to come to him. Pulling her into his arms, he held her close, brushing his lips at her temple. Holding her felt perfect. As perfect as having his daughter in his arms a moment ago. There had to be a way to make sure this wasn't the end for them. They were a family and families should be together.

His mind whirled, an idea catching hold so fast it stole his breath. Could he—?

Yes, he'd find a way.

"You need to get a move on." His voice was tight with need. "Your plane is going to be boarding soon."

Missy nodded in agreement. She got that familiar blush on her cheeks as she stared at him, clearly surprised by both his words and his actions.

Yeah, well, she hadn't seen nothing yet.

Chapter Fourteen

A video chat? Abby was freaking daft if she thought Casey was going to click on that link. Home for three days and every day there'd been a friend request she'd ignored, an email that got sent to the trash folder or now, an invite to talk face-to-face.

As if she was going to give that prissy American princess the chance to torture her from across the pond!

Hitting the cancel button gave Casey a bit of pleasure as a knock came at her bedroom door.

Her mum peeked her head inside a few seconds later. "Hey, there. Just checking in. How's the arm?"

"It's fine." Casey spun her desk chair around and studied her mum more closely, noticing how tired she looked. Was that from sitting up with her?

It was taking Casey a bit longer to get her body back on London time, and the busted arm that ached like a son of a biscuit wasn't helping. The two of them had been watching the telly late into the night, especially now that they had an on-demand streaming media account.

"How are you doing?" Casey asked.

Her mum looked down at the envelopes she held in her hand with a smile that seemed equal parts happy and sad. "I'm doing okay."

"What's that you've got?"

"Oh, just some…mail." She paused for a moment. "Old mail…your grandmum has been holding onto for me."

Casey thought her mum had gone through the stack waiting for them when they got back Monday night, but maybe she'd been wrong.

To say that things were a bit strained between her mum and Grandmum was putting it mildly. It still felt strange to be back here, knowing her grandfather was no longer around. Casey hadn't yet said anything to her grandmum about the secret her grandparents had kept from her, only because her mum had asked her not to for the time being.

"So, any big plans for the night?"

Casey thought about the chat request she'd just deleted and wondered if she should suggest it the next time she spoke with Liam. It would be great to see him again. "I don't know. I'm waiting to hear from Li—from my dad."

Her mum raised an eyebrow. "You've talked to—uh, your dad? I mean, since the first night we got back?"

"Yeah. Every day. We either text or email or he calls." She looked closer at her mum. "Is that a problem?"

"Of course not. I think it's great." She pressed the letters she held close to her chest. "Tell him h-hello from me the next time you talk."

Casey nodded, wondering about the hitch in her mum's voice but stayed quiet. And then she was alone again.

Swinging back around to her laptop, she found another video chat request, but this time it was Luke and Logan.

She grinned. Now, this one she'd accept. She missed those guys more than she'd thought she would.

When she clicked on the link, the video opened and there sat Abby.

"You!"

"Please don't hang up." Her cousin held up a hand as if she could wave off Casey's anger. "Using my brothers' names is a crappy thing to do, but I couldn't think of any other way to get you to talk to me."

It took Casey a minute, but she found the button to end the call. "I'd think you would've gotten the hint by now."

"Maybe I'm just stubborn." Abby leaned in closer, her face filling the screen. "Or maybe you knocked something loose with your right hook."

As much as she wanted to shut down the screen, Casey couldn't look away from the multicolored bruise that marred the left side of Abby's face. It ran from her brow to her jaw and Casey clenched her fingers against her cast at the memory of the pain when she hit Abby.

She hated to ask, but she had to know. "Did I…did I hurt you? The way your eye is swollen—"

"No. My eyesight is fine. It's just the outside that looks bad." Abby reached up and gingerly touched her cheek. "You should see the amount of makeup I need to cover this. I look like a cartoon character."

Casey breathed a sigh of relief that she hadn't done any damage. Then she remembered all the things Abby had done to her. "Well, what's that American saying? If the shoe fits? Look, I've got to go."

"Wait! Please, just give me five minutes."

"For what?"

"To apologize."

Surprised, Casey sat back in her chair. "You're joking."

"No, I'm not. I was a real…witch to you while you were

here. Please, feel free to respell that. I was petty and jealous—and not just because Nathan chose you over me. He really misses you, by the way, and asked me to ask you to get in touch if I ever spoke to you." Abby sighed. "Anyway, I want you to know that no one put me up to apologizing. What I did—everything I did to you—was wrong. I'm sorry."

Was this for real? Casey didn't know what to believe. Never in a million years had she expected this. Abby was a topic that she and her dad didn't talk about at all. No one really knew the bullying her cousin had done during her time in Destiny.

"Do you think it's going to be that easy?" Casey asked. "That I'm just going to forgive you?"

"No, I don't, but I wanted you to know how I feel. I know I've got…some issues. I've been talking to…someone, but apologizing is completely my idea." Abby tucked her long hair behind her ear, but then quickly pulled it back out as if trying to hide the bruising. "You should also know that everyone here misses you. Nathan, the kids at school, my brothers. My—our grandparents. And Uncle Liam—your dad, most of all. He seems really lost without you and your mom around."

Casey's throat tightened. She'd gotten that feeling too when she and her dad talked, but he never said anything.

"Look, I know you're probably ready to hit the end button on me and I wouldn't blame you. I've said what I wanted to say. I don't know if you and your mom left because of me, but I'm sure my actions made the decision easier. Again, I'm really sorry. I hope you two don't stay away from Destiny forever because of me."

The screen went blank before Casey could say anything else. Not that she had any idea how to respond to everything Abby had just said. It was nice to hear that everyone there missed them, though. As comfortable as she was being back here, surrounded by her own things, she missed her dad terribly.

She got the feeling her mum did, too.

Abby had been the one who'd told her about catching the two of them kissing on the porch and yeah, at first it had seemed a bit strange. But the more Casey had seen them together, heard about what their relationship had been like all those years ago—

The special ring chime she'd assigned to her dad filled the air.

Casey grabbed for her phone and connected the call. "Hey! I was just thinking about you."

"Well, this is good timing, then." His low-timbered voice sounded happy. "How are you doing? How's the arm?"

"I'm fine, every bit of me is. Oh, and before I forget, my mum said to say hello for her."

Silence filled the air for a moment. "She did?"

"Yep, just a few minutes ago." Casey decided the video chat between her and Abby was going to stay private for the moment.

"So, you're both at home, then?" Liam asked.

"It's almost ten o'clock on a Thursday night. Of course, we're home. Grandmum is out with her bridge club and won't be back for hours," Casey blurted out, and then bit hard on her bottom lip. That was the first time she'd mentioned her to her dad, not wanting to upset him. "I'm sorry. I didn't mean to—"

"Don't worry about it. Hey, did you get the package I sent?"

Confused, Casey looked around her room. There was nothing here. Maybe Reynolds had left it downstairs in the pantry. "No, I don't think so. Let's keep talking while I go check."

She told him about the sleepover with her friends planned for tomorrow night as she walked downstairs. Nope, nothing in the pantry, kitchen or entry table in the front hall. "I don't see anything. Do you know when it was supposed to arrive?"

"I'd think it could show up any minute. Maybe you should see if it's on your front stoop."

Casey giggled at his cryptic tone, and grabbed the door handle and pulled it open. "Well, seeing how I'm right here, let me check—Dad!"

Liam caught his daughter as she launched into his arms.

"I can't believe you're here! This is so cool!" Casey tightened her grip on him. "I've missed you so much."

Liam returned her embrace. "I've missed you, too, sweetie."

Simple words, but the truth.

It had been four long days since he'd said goodbye to her and her mother, and they had been the loneliest and emptiest days of his life.

Busy, hell, yeah, especially when he told his father and his brothers about the plan he'd come up with at the airport and fleshed out on the way home from Cheyenne the day Casey and Missy flew out. Things had been crazy around the office and they still didn't have everything figured out, but nothing compared to the ache he carried from the loss of the family he'd found with Missy and their daughter.

An ache that disappeared the moment Casey opened the door.

"Hey, you're wet. I didn't even realize it was raining. Come inside." Casey stepped back but didn't let go of him entirely as she grabbed his hand and led him inside the posh town house that spoke of the wealth and dignity of Missy's family. "Here, let me take your coat."

Liam took off his raincoat, knowing his business suit looked as if it had spent the better part of the day on an airplane, which it had. He'd stopped at his brother's flat after getting out of the airport, but only stayed long enough to greet Devlin and Tanya, drop off his suitcase, and grab a taxi.

"When did you arrive? How long are you staying? Are you here for work?"

He smiled at his daughter's rapid-fire questions. "Just a few hours ago, I don't know and no, I'm not here for work. I'm here for you."

Reaching for Casey's good hand, he held tight, knowing everything was *almost* right.

Something told him Missy was going to be a harder sell than his daughter. Still, it was important that their daughter know how he felt. "I've missed fifteen years of your life. I'm not going to miss another moment."

Casey beamed. "So is it just me or do you feel the same way about my mum?"

"Hmm, another direct question. Do you mind if I answer that by speaking directly with her?"

"Straight down the hall. Last door on the left is her office." She reached up and kissed him on the cheek. "I'll be upstairs in my room. Best of British to you!"

Liam smiled, watching her go. He didn't know exactly what she meant by that last phrase, but he guessed she was wishing him luck.

He wondered if he was going to need it.

Unlike his daily interactions with Casey, he and Missy hadn't talked once since they'd parted ways at the airport. He had no idea what kind of reception his unexpected arrival would get him. Being prepared to meet Missy's mother, Elizabeth Ellington, for the first time had him feeling like a teenager again, but it was just him and Missy here.

If she was half as happy to see him as Casey had been, he'd consider himself a winner.

Liam loved her.

At one time, he truly had, and she now had the proof she'd once so desperately needed all those years ago.

Missy sat curled up in her favorite chair, in front of a low fire, with the three long-lost letters he'd mailed her resting in her lap. Her mother had shocked her tonight when she'd handed them over before she'd headed out for the evening, as casually as if they'd arrived in the post just today.

She'd told Missy that her father had instructed her to burn them, but she never had. She'd tucked them away, just in case. Just in case the secret they'd concocted ever came to light.

What exactly her mother knew and how Missy's father had kept her quiet all these years were topics they still hadn't discussed. Only four days home and with her clothing design business exploding thanks to the princess attending a charity event in the dress she'd designed, Missy was still trying to get her spinning world under control.

A feat that seemed impossible with Liam so far away.

But now he was here—or at least the boy she'd known, the boy she'd loved, was in his letters. Finally opened, finally read. Words written in his familiar scrawl about how they'd met, how they'd fallen in love and that last terrible fight.

In the first letter, he'd begged her to come back, to find a way to forgive him for hurting her, promising they'd figure out how to be together.

The second had been more subdued. He hadn't heard from her. Did she still love him? Had anything he'd written to her meant anything? He'd told her about his victories on the rodeo circuits, but they were hollow without her there to share them.

The last one had been short, barely filling one page, written almost three months to the day after she'd left. He said he'd gotten the message. Her silence meant she'd moved on and he had to do the same. He wished her well, told her he'd never forget her and hoped she was happy.

"Happy? Am I happy?" Missy brushed the wetness from her face, her question echoing off the walls of the room. Her private sanctuary, decorated in her favorite colors, with cherished collectibles and floor-to-ceiling windows that flooded the room with natural light, even on the dreariest English rainy days. "I don't know anymore."

"Then perhaps you'll let me help."

Missy gasped at the words, the sound of his voice. She whipped around and saw the shadow of a man standing in the darkened doorway.

"I don't—you can't—" She stumbled over her own words, refusing to believe until he stepped deeper into the room. "Liam? What are you doing here?"

The small lamp on her desk was just bright enough to show his smile and the easy shrug of his powerful shoulders. He glanced down at the yellowed pages in her hand. "You never seem to get my letters. This time I decided to come in person."

"Can you believe she kept them all these years?"

He stepped farther into the room. "I'm glad you finally got to read them, but I'm here to do what I should've done before you left."

"What?"

"Tell you that I love you." He crossed the room then,

and seconds later knelt in front of her chair, his face fully lit by the glow from the fire as he took her hands in his. "That I never stopped. I'm hoping you feel the same. Tell me and we'll find a way to make this work. To be the family we—you, me and Casey—were meant to be."

"But my career… Casey's education…my mother." Her mind whirled as she tried to wrap her head around what was happening. "What about your family's business? Your career? Your life in Destiny?"

"My life is wherever you are, where you and Casey are." His fingers gave hers a gentle squeeze. "I've already started on a plan—a new one—with my dad and brothers. Restructuring within the company, spreading out job duties, digging deeper in our business interests here in the UK. Traveling to Wyoming, to wherever, as needed. My brother Devlin is heading home in a month. I plan to take over his flat, or I'll find somewhere else to stay in London. Whatever it takes, I'll do it. For you, for our daughter."

"You love me. You love Casey." Not questions this time, simple facts that made her heart soar. She didn't even have to ask, knowing he'd already stated his case to their daughter and she'd told him where to find her. "It took us a long time to find each other again."

"Too long, but we were destined to be together."

She couldn't stop from reaching for him, laying a hand on his cheek. "You were destined to be a dad."

"I already told Casey I don't want to waste another moment, miss another moment of her life. I feel the same about you. About us." Liam looked at her, his eyes bright with everything he had inside him, there for her to see. "Let me make you happy."

"You have always made me happy, Liam. The happiest I've ever been was with you," she whispered, lowering her forehead until it touched his. "I love you, my Wyoming cowboy. I always have and I always will."

* * * * *

If you liked Liam and Missy's story,
Don't miss any of
USA Today *bestselling author*
Christyne Butler's
WELCOME TO DESTINY *series.*

THE COWBOY'S SECOND CHANCE
THE SHERIFF'S SECRET WIFE
A DADDY FOR JACOBY
WELCOME HOME, BOBBY WINSLOW
HAVING ADAM'S BABY
FLIRTING WITH DESTINY
DESTINY'S LAST BACHELOR?
DESTINED TO BE A DAD

Available from Harlequin Special Edition.

From New York Times *bestselling author
Jodi Thomas comes a sweeping new series
set in a remote west Texas town—where
family can be made by blood or by choice...*

RANSOM CANYON

Staten

WHEN HER OLD hall clock chimed eleven times, Staten Kirkland left Quinn O'Grady's bed. While she slept, he dressed
in the shadows, watching her with only the light of the full
moon. She'd given him what he needed tonight, and, as
always, he felt as if he'd given her nothing.

Walking out to her porch, he studied the newly washed
earth, thinking of how empty his life was except for these
few hours he shared with Quinn. He'd never love her or
anyone, but he wished he could do something for her.
Thanks to hard work and inherited land, he was a rich man.
She was making a go of her farm, but barely. He could
help her if she'd let him. But he knew she'd never let him.

As he pulled on his boots, he thought of a dozen things
he could do around the place. Like fixing that old tractor out in the mud or modernizing her irrigation system.
The tractor had been sitting out by the road for months. If

she'd accept his help, it wouldn't take him an hour to pull the old John Deere out and get the engine running again.

Only, she wouldn't accept anything from him. He knew better than to ask.

He wasn't even sure they were friends some days. Maybe they were more. Maybe less. He looked down at his palm, remembering how she'd rubbed cream on it and worried that all they had in common was loss and the need, now and then, to touch another human being.

The screen door creaked. He turned as Quinn, wrapped in an old quilt, moved out into the night.

"I didn't mean to wake you," he said as she tiptoed across the snow-dusted porch. "I need to get back. Got eighty new yearlings coming in early." He never apologized for leaving, and he wasn't now. He was simply stating facts. With the cattle rustling going on and his plan to enlarge his herd, he might have to hire more men. As always, he felt as though he needed to be on his land and on alert.

She nodded and moved to stand in front of him.

Staten waited. They never touched after they made love. He usually left without a word, but tonight she obviously had something she wanted to say.

Another thing he probably did wrong, he thought. He never complimented her, never kissed her on the mouth, never said any words after he touched her. If she didn't make little sounds of pleasure now and then, he wouldn't have been sure he satisfied her.

Now, standing so close to her, he felt more a stranger than a lover. He knew the smell of her skin, but he had no idea what she was thinking most of the time. She knew quilting and how to make soap from her lavender. She played the piano like an angel and didn't even own a TV.

He knew ranching and watched from his recliner every game the Dallas Cowboys played.

If they ever spent over an hour talking they'd probably figure out they had nothing in common. He'd played every sport in high school, and she'd played in both the orchestra and the band. He'd collected most of his college hours online, and she'd gone all the way to New York to school. But, they'd loved the same person. Amalah had been Quinn's best friend and his one love. Only, they rarely talked about how they felt. Not anymore. Not ever really. It was too painful, he guessed, for both of them.

Tonight the air was so still, moisture hung like invisible lace. She looked to be closer to her twenties than her forties. Quinn had her own quiet kind of beauty. She always had, and he guessed she still would even when she was old.

To his surprise, she leaned in and kissed his mouth.

He watched her. "You want more?" he finally asked, figuring it was probably the dumbest thing to say to a naked woman standing two inches away from him. He had no idea what *more* would be. They always had sex once, if they had it at all, when he knocked on her door. Sometimes neither made the first move, and they just cuddled on the couch and held each other. Quinn wasn't a passionate woman. What they did was just satisfying a need that they both had now and then.

She kissed him again without saying a word. When her cheek brushed against his stubbled chin, it was wet and tasted newborn like the rain.

Slowly, Staten moved his hands under her blanket and circled her warm body, then he pulled her closer and kissed her fully like he hadn't kissed a woman since his wife died.

Her lips were soft and inviting. When he opened her mouth and invaded, it felt far more intimate than anything they had ever done, but he didn't stop. She wanted this from him, and he had no intention of denying her. No one would ever know that she was the thread that kept him together some days.

When he finally broke the kiss, Quinn was out of breath. She pressed her forehead against his jaw and he waited.

"From now on," she whispered so low he felt her words more than heard them, "when you come to see me, I need you to kiss me goodbye before you go. If I'm asleep, wake me. You don't have to say a word, but you have to kiss me."

She'd never asked him for anything. He had no intention of saying no. His hand spread across the small of her back and pulled her hard against him. "I won't forget if that's what you want." He could feel her heart pounding and knew her asking had not come easy.

She nodded. "It's what I want."

He brushed his lips over hers, loving the way she sighed as if wanting more before she pulled away.

"Good night," she said as though rationing pleasure. Stepping inside, she closed the screen door between them.

Raking his hair back, he put on his hat as he watched her fade into the shadows. The need to return was already building in him. "I'll be back Friday night if it's all right. It'll be late, I've got to visit with my grandmother and do her list of chores before I'll be free. If you like, I could bring barbecue for supper?" He felt as if he was rambling, but something needed to be said, and he had no idea what.

"And vegetables," she suggested.

He nodded. She wanted a meal, not just the meat. "I'll have them toss in sweet potato fries and okra."

She held the blanket tight as if he might see her body. She didn't meet his eyes when he added, "I enjoyed kissing you, Quinn. I look forward to doing so again."

With her head down, she nodded as she vanished into the darkness without a word.

He walked off the porch, deciding if he lived to be a hundred he'd never understand Quinn. As far as he knew, she'd never had a boyfriend when they were in school. And his wife had never told him about Quinn dating anyone special when she went to New York to that fancy music school. Now, in her forties, she'd never had a date, much less a lover that he knew of. But she hadn't been a virgin when they'd made love the first time.

Asking her about her love life seemed far too personal a question.

Climbing in his truck he forced his thoughts toward problems at the ranch. He needed to hire men; they'd lost three cattle to rustlers this month. As he planned the coming day, Staten did what he always did: he pushed Quinn to a corner of his mind, where she'd wait until he saw her again.

As he passed through the little town of Crossroads, all the businesses were closed up tight except for a gas station that stayed open twenty-four hours to handle the few travelers needing to refuel or brave enough to sample their food.

A quarter mile past the one main street of Crossroads, his truck lights flashed across four teenagers walking along the road between the Catholic church and the gas station.

Three boys and a girl. Fifteen or sixteen, Staten guessed.

For a moment the memory of Randall came to mind. He'd been about their age when he'd crashed, and he'd worn the same type of blue-and-white letter jacket that two of the boys wore tonight.

Staten slowed as he passed them. "You kids need a ride?" The lights were still on at the church, and a few cars were in the parking lot. Saturday night, Staten remembered. Members of 4-H would probably be working in the basement on projects.

One kid waved. A tall Hispanic boy named Lucas whom he thought was the oldest son of the head wrangler on the Collins Ranch. Reyes was his last name, and Staten remembered the boy being one of a dozen young kids who were often hired part-time at the ranch.

Staten had heard the kid was almost as good a wrangler as his father. The magic of working with horses must have been passed down from father to son, along with the height. Young Reyes might be lean but, thanks to working, he would be in better shape than either of the football boys. When Lucas Reyes finished high school, he'd have no trouble hiring on at any of the big ranches, including the Double K.

"No, we're fine, Mr. Kirkland," the Reyes boy said politely. "We're just walking down to the station for a Coke. Reid Collins's brother is picking us up soon."

"No crime in that, mister," a redheaded kid in a letter jacket answered. His words came fast and clipped, reminding Staten of how his son had sounded.

Volume from a boy trying to prove he was a man, Staten thought.

He couldn't see the faces of the two boys with letter jackets, but the girl kept her head up. "We've been working on a project for the fair," she answered politely. "I'm Lauren Brigman, Mr. Kirkland."

Staten nodded. *Sheriff Brigman's daughter, I remember you.* She knew enough to be polite, but it was none of his business. "Good evening, Lauren," he said. "Nice to see you again. Good luck with the project."

When he pulled away, he shook his head. Normally, he wouldn't have bothered to stop. At this rate he'd turn into a nosy old man by forty-five. It didn't seem that long ago that he and Amalah used to walk up to the gas station after meetings at the church.

Hell, maybe Quinn asking to kiss him had rattled him more than he'd thought. He needed to get his head straight. She was just a friend. A woman he turned to when the storms came. Nothing more. That was the way they both wanted it.

Until he made it back to her porch next Friday night, he had a truckload of trouble at the ranch to worry about.

Lauren

A MIDNIGHT MOON blinked its way between storm clouds as Lauren Brigman cleaned the mud off her shoes. The guys had gone inside the gas station for Cokes. She didn't really want anything to drink, but it was either walk over with the others after working on their fair projects or stay back at the church and talk to Mrs. Patterson.

Somewhere Mrs. Patterson had gotten the idea that since Lauren didn't have a mother around, she should take every opportunity to have a "girl talk" with the sheriff's daughter.

Lauren wanted to tell the old woman that she had known all the facts of life by the age of seven, and she really did not need a buddy to share her teenage years with.

Reid Collins walked out from the gas station first with a can of Coke in each hand. "I bought you one even though you said you didn't want anything to drink," he announced as he neared. "Want to lean on me while you clean your shoes?"

Lauren rolled her eyes. Since he'd grown a few inches and started working out, Reid thought he was God's gift to girls.

"Why?" she asked as she tossed the stick. "I have a

brick wall to lean on. And don't get any ideas we're on a date, Reid, just because I walked over here with you."

"I don't date sophomores," he snapped. "I'm on first string, you know. I could probably date any senior I want to. Besides, you're like a little sister, Lauren. We've known each other since you were in the first grade."

She thought of mentioning that playing first string on a football team that only had forty players total, including the coaches and water boy, wasn't any great accomplishment, but arguing with Reid would rot her brain. He'd been born rich, and he'd thought he knew everything since he'd cleared the birth canal. She feared his disease was terminal.

"If you're cold, I'll let you wear my football jacket." When she didn't comment, he bragged, "I had to reorder a bigger size after a month of working out."

She hated to, but if she didn't compliment him soon, he'd never stop begging. "You look great in the jacket, Reid. Half the seniors on the team aren't as big as you." There was nothing wrong with Reid from the neck down. In a few years he'd be a knockout with the Collins good looks and trademark rusty hair, not quite brown, not quite red. But he still wouldn't interest her.

"So, when I get my driver's license next month, do you want to take a ride?"

Lauren laughed. "You've been asking that since I was in the third grade and you got your first bike. The answer is still no. We're friends, Reid. We'll always be friends, I'm guessing."

He smiled a smile that looked as if he'd been practicing. "I know, Lauren, but I keep wanting to give you a chance now and then. You know, some guys don't want to date the sheriff's daughter, and I hate to point it out, babe, but if you don't fill out some, it's going to be bad news in college." He had the nerve to point at her chest. "From the looks of it, I seem to be the only one he'll let stand beside you, and that's just because our dads are friends."

She grinned. Reid was spoiled and conceited and self-centered, but she was right, they'd probably always be friends. Her dad was the sheriff, and his was the mayor of Crossroads, even though he lived five miles from town on one of the first ranches established near Ransom Canyon.

Tim O'Grady, Reid's eternal shadow, walked out of the station with a huge frozen drink. The clear cup showed off its red-and-yellow layers of cherry-and-pineapple-flavored sugar.

Where Reid was balanced in his build, Tim was lanky, disjointed. He seemed to be made of mismatched parts. His arms were too long. His feet seemed too big, and his wired smile barely fit in his mouth. When he took a deep draw on his drink, he staggered and held his forehead from the brain freeze.

Lucas Reyes was the last of their small group to come outside. Lucas hadn't bought anything, but he evidently was avoiding standing with her. She'd known Lucas Reyes for a few years, maybe longer, but he never talked to her. Like Reid and Tim, he was a year ahead of her, but since he rarely talked, she usually only noticed him as a background person in her world.

Unlike them, Lucas didn't have a family name following him around opening doors for a hundred miles.

Reid repeated the plan. "My brother said he'd drop Sharon off and be back for us. But if they get busy doing their thing it could be an hour. We might as well walk back and sit on the church steps."

"We could start walking toward home," Lauren suggested as she pulled a tiny flashlight from her key chain. The canyon lake wasn't more than a mile. If they walked they wouldn't be so cold. She could probably be home before Reid's dumb brother could get his lips off Sharon. If rumors were true, Sharon had very kissable lips, among other body parts.

"Better than standing around here," Reid said as Tim kicked mud toward the building. "I'd rather be walking than sitting. Plus, if we go back to the church, Mrs. Patterson will probably come out to keep us company."

Without a vote, they started walking.

Within a few yards, Reid and Tim had fallen behind and were lighting up a smoke. To her surprise, Lucas stayed beside her.

"You don't smoke?" she asked, not really expecting him to answer.

"No, can't afford the habit," he said, surprising her. "I've got plans, and they don't include lung cancer."

Maybe the dark night made it easier to talk, or maybe Lauren didn't want to feel so alone in the shadows. "I was starting to think you were a mute. We've had a few classes together, and you've never said a word. Even tonight you were the only one who didn't talk about your project."

Lucas shrugged. "Didn't see the point. I'm just entering for the prize money, not trying to save the world or build a better tomorrow."

"Hey, you two deadbeats up there!" Reid yelled. "I got an idea."

Lauren didn't want the conversation with Lucas to end, but if she ignored Reid he'd just get louder. "What?"

Reid ran up between them and put an arm over both her and Lucas's shoulders. "How about we break into the Gypsy House? I hear it's haunted by Gypsies who died a hundred years ago."

Tim caught up to them. As always, he agreed with Reid. "Look over there in the trees. The place is just waiting for us. Heard if you rattle a Gypsy's bones, the dead will speak to you." Tim's eyes glowed in the moonlight. "I had a cousin once who said he heard voices in that old place, and no one was there but him."

"This is not a good idea." Lauren tried to back away, but Reid held her shoulder tight.

"Come on, Lauren, for once in your life, do something that's not safe. No one's lived in the old place for years. How much trouble can we get into?"

"It's just a rotting old house," Lucas said so low no one heard but Lauren. "There's probably rats or rotten floors. It's an accident waiting to happen. How about you come back in the daylight, Reid, if you really want to explore the place?"

"We're all going, now," Reid announced as he shoved Lauren off the road and into the trees that blocked the view of the old homestead from passing cars. "Think of the story we'll have to tell everyone Monday. We will have explored a haunted house and lived to tell the tale."

Reason told her to protest more strongly, but at fifteen, reason wasn't as intense as the possibility of an adventure. Just once, she'd have a story to tell. Just this once…her father wouldn't find out.

They rattled across the rotting porch steps fighting tumbleweeds that stood like flimsy guards around the place. The door was locked and boarded up. The smell of decay hung in the foggy air, and a tree branch scraped against one side of the house as if whispering for them to stay back.

The old place didn't look like much. It might have been the remains of an early settlement, built solid to face the winters with no style or charm. Odds were, Gypsies never even lived in it. It appeared to be a half dugout with a second floor built on years later. The first floor was planted down into the earth a few feet, so the second floor windows were just above their heads, giving the place the look of a house that had been stepped on by a giant.

Everyone called it the Gypsy House because a group of hippies had squatted there in the Seventies. No one remembered when the hippies had moved on, or who owned the house now, but somewhere in its past a family named Stanley must have lived there because old-timers called it the Stanley house.

"I heard devil worshippers lived here years ago." Tim began making scary movie soundtrack noises. "Body parts are probably scattered in the basement. They say once Satan moves in, only the blood of a virgin will wash the place clean."

Reid's laughter sounded nervous. "That leaves me out."

Tim jabbed his friend. "You wish. I say you'll be the first to scream."

"Shut up, Tim." Reid's uneasy voice echoed in the night. "You're freaking me out. Besides, there is no basement. It's just a half dugout built into the ground, so we'll find no buried bodies."

Lauren screamed as Reid kicked a low window in, and all the guys laughed.

"You go first, Lucas," Reid ordered. "I'll stand guard."

To Lauren's surprise, Lucas slipped into the space. His feet hit the ground with a thud somewhere in the blackness.

"You next, Tim," Reid announced as if he were the commander.

"Nope. I'll go after you." All Tim's laughter had disappeared. Apparently he'd frightened himself.

"I'll go." Lauren suddenly wanted this entire adventure to be over with. With her luck, animals were wintering in the old place.

"I'll help you down." Reid lowered her into the window space.

As she moved through total darkness, her feet wouldn't quite touch the bottom. For a moment she just hung, afraid to tell Reid to drop her.

Then, she felt Lucas's hands at her waist. Slowly he took her weight.

"I'm in," she called back to Reid. He let her hands go, and she dropped against Lucas.

"You all right?" Lucas whispered near her hair.

"This was a dumb idea."

She could feel him breathing as Reid finally landed, cussing the darkness. For a moment it seemed all right for Lucas to stay close; then in a blink, he was gone from her side.

Now the tiny flashlight offered Lauren some much-needed light. The house was empty except for an old wire bed frame and a few broken stools. With Reid in the lead, they moved up rickety stairs to the second floor, where shadowy light came from big dirty windows.

Tim hesitated when the floorboards began to rock as if the entire second story were on some kind of seesaw. He backed down the steps a few feet, letting the others go first. "I don't know if this second story will hold us all." Fear rattled in his voice.

Reid laughed and teased Tim as he stomped across the second floor, making the entire room buck and pitch. "Come on up, Tim. This place is better than a fun house."

Stepping hesitantly on the upstairs floor, Lauren felt Lucas just behind her and knew he was watching over her.

Tim dropped down a few more steps, not wanting to even try.

Lucas backed against the wall between the windows, his hand still brushing Lauren's waist to keep her steady as Reid jumped to make the floor shake. The whole house seemed to moan in pain, like a hundred-year-old man standing up one arthritic joint at a time.

When Reid yelled for Tim to join them, Tim started back up the broken stairs, just before the second floor buckled and crumbled. Tim dropped out of sight as rotten lumber pinned him halfway between floors.

His scream of pain ended Reid's laughter.

In a blink, dust and boards flew as pieces of the roof rained down on them and the second floor vanished below them, board by rotting board.

COMING NEXT MONTH FROM

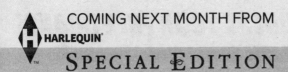

HARLEQUIN

SPECIAL EDITION

Available September 15, 2015

#2431 THE GOOD GIRL'S SECOND CHANCE
The Bravos of Justice Creek • by Christine Rimmer

Single dad Quinn Bravo and Chloe Winchester plan to spend only one night together. But the former bad boy finds he can't get the beautiful blonde out of his system that easily. Factor in his little girl, who desperately wants a mommy, and he's got the recipe for a perfect instant family!

#2432 BETTING ON THE MAVERICK
Montana Mavericks: What Happened at the Wedding?
by Cindy Kirk

When Brad Crawford wins a neighbor's ranch in a poker game, the cowboy gets more than he'd ever bargained for. Former rodeo rider Margot Sullivan, a feisty rancher's daughter, is determined to preserve her family's legacy. But what happens when love gets in the way?

#2433 ROCK-A-BYE BRIDE
The Colorado Fosters • by Tracy Madison

Anna Rockwood hadn't expected a fling with Logan Daugherty to result in a pregnancy, let alone a marriage! *She* wants real love, while *he* insists on doing the "honorable thing." But their hopes and dreams collide when they form the family of a lifetime.

#2434 THE BOSS'S MARRIAGE PLAN
Proposals & Promises • by Gina Wilkins

Scott Prince proposes marriage to his office manager, Tess Miller. He's ready to stop his family's insistent queries about his love life. Their future seems bright, but when they both develop real feelings for one another, can the bachelor find happily-ever-after with his true love?

#2435 THE TYCOON'S PROPOSAL
The Barlow Brothers • by Shirley Jump

Workaholic CEO Mac Barlow wants Savannah Hillstrand's company—and she *really* needs his business acumen. So she proposes a plan that will cater to both their interests. But what Savannah doesn't count on is the warm heart buried deep in Mac's brawny chest, or the love that will blossom in her own...

#2436 THE PUPPY PROPOSAL
Paradise Animal Clinic • by Katie Meyer

After a traumatic childhood, vet tech Jillian Everett has finally found a home in Paradise Isle, Florida. But when hotelier Nic Caruso threatens to destroy her community, Jillian is determined not to let him. So what if he's sexy *and* helps her rescue adorable dogs? That doesn't mean he's The One...or does it?

YOU CAN FIND MORE INFORMATION ON UPCOMING HARLEQUIN® TITLES, FREE EXCERPTS AND MORE AT WWW.HARLEQUIN.COM.

HSECNM0915

REQUEST YOUR FREE BOOKS!

2 FREE NOVELS PLUS 2 FREE GIFTS!

H HARLEQUIN®

SPECIAL EDITION

Life, Love & Family

SPECIAL EXCERPT FROM

HARLEQUIN®

SPECIAL EDITION

*Single dad Quinn Bravo needs a mom for his little girl...
and Chloe Winchester is the ideal candidate. But can
the former bad boy and the hometown good girl turn an
affair to remember into a forever family?*

Read on for a sneak preview of
THE GOOD GIRL'S SECOND CHANCE,
the second book in Christine Rimmer's latest miniseries,
THE BRAVOS OF JUSTICE CREEK

"I got past it."

"That doesn't make it right." At his chuckle, she chided, "It's nothing to joke about, Quinn."

He shrugged. "Tell me something."

She had that odd feeling again; there was more going on here than she was picking up. "Of course."

He let go of her hand, reached for his coffee—and said just what she'd been thinking. "Do you have any clue why I'm laying all this on you?"

She watched him take a sip. "Whatever your reasons, I have to say it's really nice to have a guy just sit right down and talk to me about the toughest things. It's rare."

"Right." He set the cup down again and rolled one of his unbuttoned cuffs to the elbow. "It's what women love. A guy who won't shut up…"

"I don't know about 'women.' But I know what *I* like. And you telling me about what matters to you, about what made you who you are? I do like that. A lot."

"Well, all right." He rolled the other cuff. She watched him, admiring the hard shape of his arms, thick with muscle, roped with tendons, dusted with light brown hair, nicked here and there with small white ridges of scar tissue. He went on, "But I do have a reason for loading you up with way more info than you asked for."

"And I keep trying to make you see that you don't *need* a reason."

He slanted her a teasing look. "Got that."

A low laugh escaped her. "Well, okay, then. I get it. You're trying to tell me the reason—so go ahead. I'm ready for it."

"You sure?"

She groaned and executed a major eye roll. "Will you *please* stop teasing me?"

Now he looked at her so steadily, a look that made her warm all over, especially down in the center of her. "All right." And then, just like that, he said, "I want to marry you, Chloe."

HARLEQUIN
SPECIAL EDITION

Life, Love and Family

Sit, Stay…Fall In Love?

After a traumatic childhood, vet tech Jillian Everett has finally found a home in Paradise Isle, Florida. But when hotelier Nic Caruso threatens to destroy her community, Jillian is determined not to let him. So what if he's sexy *and* helps her rescue adorable dogs? That doesn't mean he's The One…or does it?

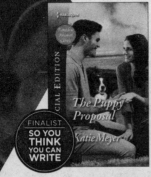

SAVE $1.00

on the purchase of THE PUPPY PROPOSAL by Katie Meyer
{available Sept. 15, 2015} or any other Harlequin® Special Edition book.

Redeemable at participating outlets in the U.S. and Canada only. Not redeemable at Barnes & Noble stores. Limit one coupon per customer.